A MAN NAMED
CULLY

ORRIS SLADE

CONTENTS

CHAPTER 1

Samuel "Cully" McCullough would have preferred to stay in Cortez and see hang the two murderers he brought in to the sheriff. Not that he enjoyed hangings, but the two outlaws deserved their fate. However, he was expected back in Pueblo. With some regret, he slung his leg over his saddle and headed south.

He rode past green and brown scenery along the way and spied a herd of elk trudging along in a wooden area. He had to admit the journey from Cortez to Pueblo was a pleasant one. The sight of the two men dangling from a rope would have been less aesthetically pleasing but more satisfying. The two had invaded a small farm near Woodhill and killed the couple that lived there, stole anything worth stealing, and then set the house on fire. Cully could discover no reason for the crime except pure meanness. But the Mendez brothers were known for their meanness and their savagery. He had been invited by the Cortez sheriff, Bodie Smith to watch the brothers' short drop into a long darkness. He thanked Smith but said he had to get back to Pueblo.

He had witnessed hangings before. They were quick, final, and bloodless. The convicted men didn't die of strangulation as some people thought. The drop almost always broke their necks, and they died instantly.

The trail was straight. He had traveled it before. A deer scampered across his path. He heard rustling of small animals in the brush. Squirrels scampered from tree to tree. A smaller animal peered from behind a dark green bush.

Cully shook away the fatigue and thought he would bed down for an hour or so before continuing the journey. His horse, Samson, was strong. Samson had rested for a day and was well fed and groomed before they started the journey. But Cully hadn't rested much when he was in Cortez. He eased Samson into some trees and climbed down. He leaned back on a trunk of a tree, his hat over his eyes. He was dozing within minutes.

The shot woke him. Samson neighed and jerked his head up. If Cully needed another wake up call, three more shots sounded. Shouts also came his way. Mean, ugly shouts. The voices had a nastiness to them.

"Samson, let's see what's going on," Cully said.

He quickly mounted and spurred Samson toward the noise. When Samson galloped over the hill, he spied the covered wagon with three young cowboys circling it and howling like bloodthirsty savages. The fourth man pointed his gun at a family standing against the wagon. A man, woman, and three children. The girl looked the oldest. She was taller than the two boys. A dog was tied to the wagon with a leash. He growled at the riders. The gunman stood about five feet away from the family. He wore a hideous grin as if he was enjoying the spectacle.

Cully galloped toward the wagon from the south so quickly, he caught the four men off guard. The gunman realized a horse was coming his way but paid no attention to it. In five seconds, he realized his mistake.

Cully bore down on him with his fifteen hundred pound horse. Samson barreled into the man, tossing him ten feet into the air. He landed solidly on the hard, black ground and groaned. He tried to roll over, but his arms and legs lacked the strength. His gun turned over in the air and plopped into the brush. Cully turned his horse to face the other three cowboys. They rode toward him then stopped. What looked to be the youngest man put his hand on his gun.

"I don't know who you are, mister, but you better mind your own business," he said.

"This is my business. I've had a couple of real busy days, and I was napping when your caterwauling woke me up. You coots were yelling like stuck pigs."

The cowboy blinked and sat back in his saddle. He dropped his voice. "It's none of your business."

Cully smiled. He had a deep baritone voice that always commanded attention. "Yes, it is. That gentleman you were holding a gun on is my fifty-fifth cousin. He and his family are relatives." The deep voice dropped to an even deeper tone, tinged with anger. "I don't like people threatening my kin."

The cowboy pulled his horse back several steps. Now he was in line with his two friends. "In case you haven't noticed, there are three of us and only one of you."

"There were four of you a short time ago. I've handled three before. I've handled professionals—not green-willowed, yellow-bellied sapsuckers like you. You've got two choices. You drop your guns and hightail out of here or fill your hand. If you do the latter you'll be in a grave before the sun sets."

"You talk big," the cowboy said.

"No. I am big. I talk hard and straight. You have five seconds to make your choice."

The cowboy's hand was next to his holster. He stiffened then drew. His gun hadn't cleared leather when Cully's bullet slammed into his chest above the heart. A second bullet blasted skin an inch under the first shot. The cowboy wobbled in the saddle, then he lowered his head and fell to the ground. His two friends threw up their hands.

"Don't shoot!" one yelled.

"OK, you varmints. Very slowly reach down and unbuckle your gun belts and let them drop to the ground."

Cully watched as the two men did exactly as he said. With his left hand, he moved his vest over so the two could see the silver star on his shirt. "There's something I forgot to tell you. I'm a United States Federal Marshal and you have interfered with my business. I could arrest you for that. But I'm going to say you just fell in with bad company." With his gun, he gestured to the dead man on the ground. "But he's dead now, so there's no more bad company to fall in with." His voice hardened. "But you two get out of this county and get out of this state. Now git!"

The two men turned their horses around and galloped away. Cully watched them until they were out of sight. Then he smiled and holstered his gun. He turned his horse around and looked at the settlers.

"Hello, cousin," he said. "Good to see you."

The man walked up to him and offered his hand. "Alexander Harris. I'm glad to meet you. Always nice to meet a long-lost cousin."

Cully smiled and shook Harris's hand. "You can call me Cully."

"That's my wife, Mary, and my daughter, Katie, with sons, Matthew and Peter. The dog who is no longer growling is Captain. He has a much higher rank than I did when I was in the army. I'm glad you were passing by."

Cully tipped his hat to Harris's wife. "I always try to be at the right place at the right time."

The woman walked over and offered her hand too. "Like my husband, I'm very glad you came by, Mr. Cully."

"I didn't realize guns would be needed on the trip," Harris said. "I came here without one. A handgun, that is. I had a rifle, but when the four came up, they looked friendly. Then one grabbed my rifle, and the other three drew their guns."

"They give a reason for hassling you?"

"Said their boss didn't like homesteaders and told us to go back east."

Cully nodded. At one time, a few large cattlemen had, for the most part, a great deal of open rangeland to themselves. They grazed their cattle on it. Now many people were moving in from the east, setting up ranches or farms, and using barbed wire to line their property, reducing the amount of land the cattlemen could use for, basically, almost free grazing land. "Did they say who they were employed by?"

"No."

"Well, wouldn't take a hard guess. There are only three or four cattlemen who have big ranches in this area. Has to be one of them."

"Mr. Cully, we're on our way to our farm. It's only about five miles from here," Mary Harris said. "We'd like to invite you to dinner. How long has it been since you had a home-cooked meal?"

"Thank you, ma'am. I need to get back to Pueblo, but I'm not going to ride at night. To be honest, my stomach is telling me it's been way too long since I've had a good meal. I appreciate the invitation."

"Just follow along with us," Harris said. "It won't take long to get to the house."

Within minutes the children were back in the wagon while Harris and Mary drove the horses. Cully rode alongside. Samson trotted easily over the grassy land. The orange sun behind the high snowcapped mountains gave an orange glow to the horizon. Cully had seen sunsets before, many of them, but he admitted all of them were not only beautiful but also gave off a sense of awe. He was the son of a minister, the deceased Reverend Benjamin McCullough, but he had gradually moved away from the faith. Watching the sun set, Cully felt a tug to return to his spiritual home. To him, the incredible beauty of the West—the mountains, the valleys, the majestic continental divide—did speak of God. *If you have not stood near a lake while a burnt orange sun eases down to the horizon, spreading misty orange light across rippling waters, you have not fully lived*, Cully thought. If you have not seen the magnificent mountains that speak of splendor and majesty, then there is an emptiness in your life, he believed. The late Reverend McCullough had noted you can see signs of creation in nature. Cully agreed with his father on that theological point.

Mary Harris's voice broke into his thoughts. "How long have you been a U. S. Marshal, Cully?"

"This time about fifteen days, ma'am. It's an off and on profession."

"Really?"

He smiled. "I grew up in the country. I know about guns, and I know about hunting. I feel at home in the forest and always a bit uncomfortable in towns. I hunted a lot of animals. And I've hunted men too."

Mary looked a bit shocked. "You were a bounty hunter?"

"Yep. To be honest, private work pays better than being a Federal Marshal does."

"Why did you become a bounty hunter?"

His dark eyes became darker. She had noticed the tall, brown stranger with the deep voice was stoic, but he did smile a lot. He didn't smile now. And the voice stayed emotionless as he told the tale.

"My father was a minister. My mother was a wonderful woman and loved everyone. When I was sixteen, a gang of outlaws rode into our town. They had planned to rob the bank, but their escape became a hail of gunfire when they tried to get out of town. My father was gunned down and died on the streets. Some horses, spooked by all the noise, galloped down the main street to get away from the noise. Mother was turning a corner when the horses trampled her."

"Oh, no."

"When I turned eighteen, I swore an oath to the god my father believed in that I would rid the earth of scum like the outlaws who killed my parents. Bounty hunting allowed me to do that. I didn't bother with the thieves. Or the low-level criminals. I leave them to men with badges. I took on the murderers, the wolves who preyed on sheep. I evened the odds. Most people don't cotton to bounty hunters, and I can understand that. But I never regretted my work. I love animals, and I love dogs. But if one goes rabid, you have to kill him. Same thing with men. Criminals do not need to be running around loose. I hogtie the varmints, then bring them in. If they surrender that is."

"And if they don't surrender?"

"The cemetery gets a new grave, ma'am. I pay two dollars for their funeral after I get my bounty money. Don't want them to be a burden for the taxpayers, so I pay for six feet of their final resting place."

"So why become a Federal Marshal?"

"A friend of mine is Marshal Tate Buchanan. Been friends with Tate for years. When he needs an extra man, I help him out. I'm a man who stands by his friends." He gave a quick grin. "Even when it costs me money."

CHAPTER 2

The Harris's ranch was a roomy one-story residence with a barn, a corral, and a green pasture on slanted land that ran to a bubbling creek. The boys told Cully they often fished there and asked if he wanted to cast a line into the flowing stream. It was not lacking in fish; they said. Cully thanked them but said although he would like to, he had no time for fishing.

Dinner was roast beef with luscious gravy, potatoes, and buttered corn. It was one of the best meals Cully had ever eaten. He complimented the chefs. After dinner, Harris went outside to smoke his pipe. Cully followed him. The stars shone a silver light on the land as the two stood outside the house. Harris flicked a match and lit his pipe. Gray smoke filled the air as did the aroma of tobacco.

"In a hurry to get back to Pueblo, Cully?" he said.

"Not personally. Did get a telegram saying I was needed back there. It was signed by one of Tate's fellow marshals, a man named Virgil Hagin. I know him, although not as well as I know Tate, but he's a nice guy and a good sheriff. I don't know what he wants, but I think I need to get back there as soon as possible."

"Thanks again for the help today. I don't want to think what might have happened if you hadn't come along."

"I don't think they intended to kill you, but in situations like that, you can't tell what might happen. The friction between the large ranchers and settlers is increasing. I'm hearing more and more reports of violence."

Harris nodded. "I've heard some rumbling myself. But the ranchers just have to accept the state is not theirs. They have to share it with others. There's enough land for everyone."

Cully nodded as well. "I don't doubt it, but there are a few men who disagree with that view. They want all the land, or all the grazing land, and they don't want fences. There is enough land to go around, but some men are greedy. Fortunes can be made and lost out here, and greed can bring out the worst in men."

"Well, all I want is a patch of land where I can plant and grow and make a good living for my family."

———

Before Cully went to bed, he unsaddled his horse and tied Samson near the water trough at the back of the house. He gave him enough rope to roam a bit. He grabbed his rifle and took it inside. He didn't like to be too far from his rifle even though he wore a sidearm. The family had a spare room, and after saying good night to them, he stretched out on the bed. He had been traveling for weeks and hadn't slept in a bed for a while. A mattress, he decided, was better than hard ground for sleeping.

The bark of a dog woke him. He sensed it was several hours after midnight. Cully was not a man who stayed drowsy whether he woke up in the middle of the night or in the early morning hours. He usually woke at dawn, wide awake when his feet hit the floor. Now, he was just as awake when his fingers touched his rifle. The dog barked again. He heard it running in the house. He pulled on his boots and ran from his bedroom. The dog barked again and raced from the front of the house to the back.

"It's all right," Cully said, and somehow the deep but confident voice calmed the dog. He emitted only a low howl. Cully petted him.

Harris walked in from the hall, a rifle in his hand. He went to the window and looked out. "Don't see anything but it's pitch dark outside. We trained Captain as a watchdog. If he's barking, there's something out there sneaking around."

"You have a back door?" Cully asked.

Harris nodded.

"Then I'm going to slip out. Lock and bolt it behind me. Shove something behind it so it's secure."

"You sure you know what you're doing?"

Cully smiled. "Yes, I've been a hunter and tracker all my life. I've tracked men at night. A mountain lion has nothing on me, even when I'm on the plains."

The two walked to the back door. Cully opened it slightly and peeked out. He saw nothing and heard nothing. And like the mountain lion, he sensed safety.

"I think everybody's out in front."

"You think it's men."

"Yes, maybe those men who attacked you earlier today have a few black sheep cousins."

Cully dashed out the door. Harris slammed it shut.

Running smoothly and easily, Cully circled the house. He found a spot about fifty feet from it. The house was on a slight incline which allowed participants to stare out over the land. Cully stretched out on top of the small hill and looked toward a batch of trees and brush about a hundred yards from the cabin. If attackers wanted to charge the cabin, they'd have a hundred yards of open ground to cover. Not wise if a dog had just woken up the occupants. He focused his gaze at the edge of the clearing. He stayed still for five minutes then thought he saw movement. A glint in the moonlight. Then a second movement. A shadow that moved when it shouldn't have. There was no wind, and no reason a shadow should move in the breeze, unless it could walk.

Another glint. Only a half moon was in the sky, but it gave Cully enough light to see glimmers of three men and a rifle sticking out from the brush.

The rifle spit fire. Cully saw a flash and heard the bullet hit the wall of the cabin. Two other rifles appeared, and both fired.

Cully aimed his own gun. It was not an easy shot, not in the dark, but Cully was a good marksman. He pulled the trigger three times. Bullets whizzed toward his targets. He thought he heard a groan, and one silver rifle dropped to the ground.

"Listen to me, you low down polecats. I know you're there. You better listen and listen good!"

He waited a moment. Nothing moved. The rifles disappeared from the brush.

"If you were expecting to be up against a sodbuster who is a lousy shot, you're mistaken. I am a U.S. Federal Marshal, and you scalawags better git! My mama told me to be polite and always give a warning before I put holes in a man's hide.

So I'm giving you fair warning. Unless you're good at night fighting, you better jump on your horses and hightail it. If not, you won't live to see the sunrise. You've got about thirty seconds to decide. You throw those guns out and head for Texas."

It took about thirty seconds for the hidden men to respond. They didn't throw out their weapons. Two silver rifles fired, but the bullets didn't come close to Cully. They raced through the air or hit dirt twenty yards from him.

Cully gave a bitter snort. These men were not professionals, not gunmen for hire. Just range scalawags who needed money and didn't care how they got it. Even so, they fired into a house with a woman and three children. They deserved no sympathy, he thought. He shook his head. He really did not want to kill them, but he was going to protect the Harris family.

He yelled again, "For the sake of my dear mother, bless her soul, I'll give you one last warning. Ride away! This is your last chance." If you stay, he thought, my conscience is clear.

More fire spit from the rifles.

"Well, you asked for it," he said, raising his rifle. A friend who was also a Civil War veteran had brought him a repeating rifle, introduced during the last year of the war. Cully rapidly fired. Seven shots tore through the bushes. Another rifle was dropped and stayed on the ground. A good sign, Cully thought.

He moved quickly but silently as he circled into the bush but moved around toward his targets. He smiled as he recalled another friend, a man who had no sense of direction. The man could get lost walking across the street. Cully always knew where he was and how to get to his destination. He couldn't see the brush where the men had fired toward the house, but he sensed where it was. In two minutes he was in the forest behind the attackers. He heard a rustling and voices.

"We've got to get away."

"No, going to kill him."

"Rusty, Jack is wounded. You took a bullet in your side."

Due to the moonlight, Cully could make out three figures. One held a pistol. Another a rifle.

"Been shot before. I can take it. Gonna kill that man."

Cully's baritone voice startled the two men. "No, you're not! Throw your guns down!"

In the shadows, the two men stared at one another. A mistake, Cully thought. A moment of indecision. You can't do that and expect to survive. Not in the West. You have to think and act quickly. It was only a moment, but that was enough. The man with the rifle turned swiftly and tried to aim. Cully's bullets caught the rifleman in the chest. He pitched back, letting the rifle fall to the ground. Blood and skin flew through the air.

The second man had to pivot to aim his pistol at Cully. But he too had a moment of hesitation. Before he could fire, Cully's bullet smashed into his shoulder. His gun dropped from his hand. He groaned. His wobbly legs wouldn't support him. They weakened, and he slipped to his knees, one hand over the wound. Blood leaked between his fingers. As Cully walked past him, he slammed the butt of his rifle across the man's head, so he slumped to the ground and didn't move.

The third man bled from a wound to his side. He leaned against a tree and raised both hands as far as he could. "Don't shoot," he said.

"If you want to go three on one again, you should pick better partners. What's your name?"

"Jack Trahane."

"Well, Jack, I hope Mr. Harris has a buckboard. I'm going to haul you into town and, after a trip to the local doctor, take you to the sheriff's office. And you're going to tell the sheriff who hired you." He lowered the rifle and pointed it between Trahane's eyes. "You understand?"

Trahane swallowed and nodded.

"And you're not going to give me any trouble on the way there, are you?"

Trahane shook his head.

"Not that you could if you wanted to," Cully said. "Get up. Think I will keep an eye on you while we get the buckboard hitched up. We'll leave your friend here and pick him up when we travel to town. Jack, if you're lucky you will be able to use your arm again. If not, it'll be a reminder you shouldn't shoot at innocent folks, especially women and children."

"We didn't know there were women and children in the house," Trahane said, a defiant tone coming into his voice. "I wouldn't shoot a woman or a child. We were told a sodbuster built a cabin on Mr. Jackson's land, and Jackson wanted him hit."

"This Mr. Jackson… He wanted the sodbuster dead or run out of the county?"

Trahane said nothing for a minute. "We didn't know there was a woman and children involved."

Cully's voice was not only strong but indignant. "Then you have even more reason to tell the sheriff about your employer. He lied to you, or at least was not honest with you. So you should have no problem telling the sheriff about him. He really should have mentioned that Mr. Harris was not alone in the house. A dog was there too. But you and the sheriff can sort that out." He smiled. "I'll say hello and then be on my way to Pueblo."

CHAPTER 3

The deserted, ramshackle two-story house a half mile from the outskirts of Durango looked uninviting. And with the decaying wood and columns, it looked as if a stiff wind would blow it down. But to Horace "Smiley" James, the broken-down house was a gold mine. Although his face was on numerous wanted posters for various crimes, including murder, Smiley was, in fact, smiling today. He had a plan that would make him rich without him having to risk his neck. He also knew he had to lie low for a while and keep out of sight. He knew there were a great many wanted posters in this section of Colorado showing his face. He was going to grow a mustache and beard. That would help. For he was going to hide almost in plain sight. He was going to establish a business, a business that had been profitable for as long as men liked women.

Smiley had manners—or he could pretend to have manners—but no morals. He was cunning but not honest. Dedicated but with no sense of decency. But Smiley liked to believe he thought big, and he was about to prove it. He was wanted for a number of robberies. He had robbed banks, stagecoaches, and one train. His gang was professional and loyal, and they didn't question him. The last gang member who did, a man named Mike Hartman, paid for his insolence. Smiley shot him between the eyes.

But robbing banks or trains had a downside. There was a risk of being shot, plus the risk of getting your face pasted on a wanted poster. There was a $1,000 reward for him, dead or alive. He also knew there were any number of bounty hunters in the area, and they would not waste time bringing him in alive if they could just sling his body over a horse and bring him in dead. He understood perfectly the bounty hunters' point of view. Smiley didn't mind shooting a man in the back. He always thought the concept of a fair fight was dumb. You could get killed in a fair fight. Shooting a man in the back lowered the chances of getting killed. He knew some bounty hunters had his own sense of fairness and wouldn't bother asking him to come with them peacefully. They would just shoot him and collect the reward.

So he was going to become a businessman, a disreputable businessman to be sure, and a businessman who usually stayed in his own building during the day, but a businessman never the less.

He walked to the door when he heard the wagon roll up. The driver stopped at a side door. Smiley opened the door and watched as two men hustled the bundle out of the wagon. It was clearly a body wrapped in a blanket. They walked quickly and entered the building. Smiley halted them and pulled the blanket down. He saw a young woman, a brunette with small features, eyes closed.

"You use the chloroform? She looks dead. I need her alive."

"She'll be fine, Boss. I used just enough," said Christopher "Lucky Lynn," one of his gang. "I worked in a hospital some years ago. I know how much to use. She may be out for a couple of hours, but she'll be fine."

Smiley nodded. "Good. Take her to the second floor. Make sure you lock the door." He put the blanket back over her face. His gang had gathered around him. In addition to Lucky, there was Jake "The Snake" Baxter, Manuel "Mudsy" Woods, and Jasper Palmer. Palmer was the one man who had not picked up a nickname. All were dependable, but they had to be kept in line. He raised his hand and pointed a finger at them.

"I'm going to be out getting things organized. You all remember I get the first sampling. That will be the case with all the women. You will leave her alone. You don't touch her until I get back, and then I go first. If you don't, I'll skin you, salt your hide, and hang it from a barn door. Understand?" Smiley said.

Every man nodded.

"OK. Palmer, you're the cook. You actually cook meals that can be eaten. You'll buy some food while I'm gone and set up a kitchen. We're going to build a bar too, so our customers can drink while they're waiting."

"What are we going to do while you're gone, Boss?" Lucky said.

"You are going to be busy. You are going to be cleaning."

"Cleaning? Boss, we're outlaws."

"You're whatever I say you are," Smiley said, a gruff tone coming into his voice. "We can't have a dusty, dirty house, and this place needs a good cleaning. You will have to buy some brooms and mops and whatever people use to clean nowadays. I will also have to find out where we can get some beds shipped.

"Boys, we are going to have a nice, pleasant house that serves drinks and maybe even a little food. A very high-class place. And we are going to charge the maximum for our services. I not only want customers from Pueblo, I want customers from the surrounding counties to ride over and enjoy our hospitality. No more risking our necks, no more getting shot at. We won't have to ride after money. The money will come to us.

"But first we have some planning to do—and some cleaning. When I get back, I want the house spick-and-span, sparkling clean. We are going to give our customers the best. Have to get some furniture too if our customers have to wait. But before I go, we have to get some ladies to help."

"Women are kind of scarce around here, Boss," Lucky said. "And the ones we do have around are fat and ugly. I've seen one or two that would have to pay me, not the other way around."

"I have thought about that, and I have a solution."

"Really? Smiley, we can't go around kidnapping women. I know you have one upstairs, but that's very risky. Sooner or later someone will spot us, and we'll have a dozen lawmen on our tails. And we can't lead them back to this house or the whole business goes down the drain."

Smiley showed a huge grin. He had already begun to think of himself as a fine-dressed businessman, not an outlaw or kidnapper or killer. People would soon step aside when he walked down the street, not because of his gun but because of his influence and respectability. He thought he'd like to be called Mr. James by most folks. Only a few special friends would get to call him Smiley in the future.

"Palmer, you're a very good outlaw but you must have no imagination. We will not be out kidnapping women, which as you noted is a very dangerous activity. The lady upstairs is an exception to the rule. But we will not have to go hunt for ladies. They will come to us as nice as you please."

"They will?"

"Absolutely," Smiley said.

"Boss, I don't know what your plan is, but it has to a doozy. You're right, I have no imagination. I cannot imagine women coming up to our door, knocking politely, and saying hello. You'll have to explain that to me. I knew you were smart, Boss, but I didn't know you were a genius."

"Actually, it's very easy. I assume you have heard of mail-order brides."

"Sure have."

Smiley had folded up a newspaper and stuck it in his hip pocket. He reached for it and unfolded it. "Have you heard of the *Matrimonial Times*?"

"Can't say I have, but I don't read much, and I've never been much for matrimony."

"What's matrimony?" asked Mudsy.

"Marriage."

"Oh, never been much for that, either."

Smiley waved the paper at them. "The *Matrimonial Times*, my criminal friends, is a paper dedicated to love and marriage. Young ladies in the East flock to it like flies to honey. Those ladies are looking for a husband, and they write charming letters telling would be suitors why they would be wives. And men in the West, who can't find a woman out here due to the fact that there aren't a whole lot of women out here, write about how they would be a good husband. They often mention their business or ranch or farm to show the women they would be a good provider. It's a marriage made in heaven or in the newspaper."

"But what does that have to do with us?"

"Because a certain Luther Malone has written for a mail-order bride. He claims to be a rancher located just outside Pueblo and…" Smiley opened the newspaper to a page and tapped an item. "He claims to have a rather good-sized ranch, one that would provide a wife with a very good living."

"Who cares if a guy named Luther Malone has a ranch?"

"Because Luther Malone is me. I wrote the advertisement and, if I say so myself, gave myself a very impressive background. I'm a successful rancher who only lacks one thing in life: a wife."

Lucky frowned. "Boss, you lost me. Are there actually women who would believe that? And, if there are, who cares?"

"Actually, I'm glad you asked that, Lucky. A young lady from Philadelphia named Susie Thomas has replied to the ad and is at this moment on her way to the train station in Denver to meet her charming future husband. Lucky, you will meet the young lady and bring her here, going along with the story for a while, of course. You will be about two days on the trail, but she is not to be harmed or touched. You understand?"

Lucky nodded. "I don't consider myself a stupid man, but it's beginning to dawn on me, Boss. Instead of going to a ranch, she comes here and works for us. Or dies."

"Very perceptive, Lucky. That is how we get other ladies to this place. I have written a few other mail-order bride advertisements. My description of my looks was not too accurate, but then I asked the young lady to describe herself since I describe myself. We should have a sampling to pick from. You get to meet the young ladies when they get off the train, Lucky. Of course we are going to have to pretty you up."

"What?" Lucky frowned.

"Lucky, you are no longer an outlaw varmint running from the law. When you're not chewing out your friends here, you can speak well. You will speak well when you meet the young lady. I don't want her suspicious in a train station. A train station is public, and there's a lot of people around. If she smells a trap, she doesn't have to come with you, and you can't kidnap her in public. If you tried, you'd be in the city jail."

"I get your drift, Boss, but I haven't had much practice being diplomatic."

"You don't have to be diplomatic, just friendly. But we are going to get you tidied up. You're going to get a haircut today, and a bath, and buy some new clothes. Shave too. You have a two-day beard. You can curse a blue streak, Lucky, but you can talk nice if you have to, and for the young lady, you have to."

This was not Smiley's first trip to the boarding house. He had made previous trips to stock up supplies. He moved to a shelf and grabbed the whiskey bottle sitting there. He placed it on the table, then found five glasses and poured whiskey into them.

"Gentlemen, to be bluntly honest, the lifespan for members of the profession we are in is not high. Ever seen an old outlaw?"

"After they got out of prison," Palmer said.

"Exactly. Most die young. So if we expect to live long lives and have money to enjoy life, we need to change professions. I am going to become a prosperous businessman, and you will be my associates." He raised his glass for a toast. The other men clinked their glasses on his.

"Gentlemen, in our new profession we will look nice, we will smell sweet, we will smile at others. No brawling. No fighting. We keep smiling." Smiley dropped his voice. "But if any man or woman gets in our way, we kill them. Any lawmen snoop around here, he goes under the ground. If a woman gives us too much trouble, we bop her on the head and bury her outside. If anyone interferes with us, we shoot them."

"But we shoot them with a smile, right, Boss?" Lucky said.

"Couldn't have said it better myself."

———

As the train's wheels rattled over the tracks, Susie Thomas looked out of the window with a degree of apprehension. She had left her family—her mother and father and mean older brother—to come to Colorado, where she didn't know a soul. During the hours of the train ride, she asked questions to herself, wondering if she was doing the right thing. But she thought her life in Pennsylvania was a dead end, with blackness at every corner.

Her father had desired a second son and was profoundly disappointed when Susie turned out to be a girl. She encountered his displeasure almost every day. She had never received any love from her father. He had never told her he loved her or even hugged her. Her mother wasn't much better although at times she did say soft and gentle words to her daughter. Her older brother had all the negative traits of her father.

She had thought there was some degree of home when she met Sherman Kane. They enjoyed one another's company and seemed to meld together. Susie had learned to knit from her mother, and they knitted several quilts together. In the quilts, the colors blended. All the different shades wove together beautifully. She thought she and Sherman had melded together, too, but his family was well-to-do and her family was poor. His parents had made clear they wanted their son to have nothing to do with the girl who lived on the wrong side of the bank accounts. The only hope, she thought, was to get away, go some place where she could start anew.

That is why she picked up the *Matrimonial Times* and read the advertisements of Western men for mail-order brides. A man, Luther Malone, seemed to be the type of man she needed. He had a good-sized ranch near Pueblo, Colorado, and he promised a good life. He said he had worked hard all his life—he was thirty-one years old—and had become successful. But he said there were not that many women in the West, and he desired a wife. He had a house, but he needed a wife to make the house a home.

Susie had kept his letters. She had one in her handbag and the others in her suitcase. They were sweet and flowery but a bit awkward as if the writer wasn't used to writing. The English seemed a bit stifled and occasionally a wrong word was used. Mr. Malone must have understood that, because he apologized in advance for the writing, noting he had spent most of his time building up his ranch and not too much time writing.

One item that did interest her was that Mr. Malone noted he had several horses on the ranch, a large corral and plenty of space to ride. Of the three he said there was a gentle white gelding on his barn, getting fat on hay. Adele, the gelding, needed some exercise.

Susie had been on a horse only one time, but she really enjoyed the experience. She liked horses the way some people like dogs. She wanted to care for a few. The home she grew up in was small—very small. She longed to see the riding space on Mr. Malone's ranch.

The ranch had a big house too. She would enjoy that. She would have room to walk around. She had mentioned in her letters that she liked to read, and Malone had promised she would have a study in the house, all to herself. She could read, write, or just gaze at the green, rolling hills on the ranch. She embraced that.

There was no privacy in her childhood home. In Colorado, she would have a room to herself just to read or think. Possibly think about how fortunate she was to get out of

Philadelphia. The study would also be a place to write her best friend, Lottie Raulerson.

Lottie, like her, came from an unhappy home, but unlike her, Lottie's parents did have some money. They were not rich, but the income was moderate and took care of all the needs of the household. However, it was fortunate that liquor did not cost a lot, or Lottie's father would have spent all the family's savings on the bottle. The two had become fast friends and Lottie encouraged her to make the break from her family and Philadelphia. Lottie was a bit concerned about the letters. They seemed a bit incoherent to her. The letters rambled some, she thought. Susie said that was just because Mr. Malone was not a polished writer.

She regretted she had not told Sherman she was leaving. But she knew his family would never permit the marriage. She didn't want to see him again, because if she did, it would be difficult—if not impossible—to leave him. She could picture herself hanging onto him and telling him not to leave her. But the gap between his family and hers was too much. A tear came to her eye and eased down her cheek as she thought about him. She shook her head. He was a fine man. She wished him well. She wished things could have been different.

She shook her head again and wiped away the tear. She couldn't think anymore of Sherman. She had a new life in Colorado. On a beautiful ranch. She could write to him and explain and tell him, very truthfully, that she wished him well and hoped he had a happy life.

CHAPTER 4

Lottie Raulerson raced to the door to stop the fervid knocking. She was afraid it would rock the door off the hinges. For a moment she wondered if the man knocking was drunk. "Who is it?" she asked tentatively.

"Sherman Kane."

Usually, she wouldn't have opened the door to a man when her parents were not home, but she knew Kane and liked him. She reached for the doorknob and turned it. "Don't break your fingers, Mr. Kane," she said. "What is it?"

Kane was a good-looking man, tall and muscled, with neatly combed black hair. She always thought he had a confident look.

But not today. The black hair was no longer neatly combed. Strands ran in all directions. He must have run to her house because he appeared to be out of breath. His dark eyes looked apprehensive if not fearful.

"Miss Raulerson, do you know what happened to Miss Thomas? I went by her house, but she wasn't there. I must find her!" There was an urgency in his voice.

"Mr. Kane, didn't she tell you?"

"No, she told me nothing. What are you talking about?"

"Come in, come in."

Kane rushed in and sat in a chair.

Lottie eased down on a sofa. "Mr. Kane, Susie answered a reply for a mail-order bride from a man in Colorado. She said your parents hated her, and there was no hope for you and her. She said your parents would never let you marry her."

Fury came into Kane's eyes. He bristled with indignation. "My parents can't tell me who to marry or who not to marry. They had told me their view of the marriage, and I have told them mine. I told them I plan to propose to Susie because I love her and want her as my wife. I also told them I didn't care if they object or not. If they want to keep me as their son, they should accept my decision and not just accept Susie but welcome her into the family."

"What did they say?" Lottie asked.

"They were stunned and have not yet given me an official reply. Which is immaterial."

"Mr. Kane, I'm so sorry. I know Susie loved you and wanted to marry you. But she thought that was impossible. So she answered the letter and was asked to come to Colorado. I think she's on a train right now."

"Oh, no." He made a fist. "I will go after her. I'll find her. It's my fault she left. I should have told her I didn't care what my parents thought."

"Susie told me your parents could cut off all your money. She said, 'No man will marry a bride who will make him penniless.'"

Kane brushed away the words the way you would brush away a fly. "It's true my parents have money. That's no secret. Some money is in their name, of course, and they have other accounts that I would inherit in a year or so. But I have my own money, and I've taken good care of it. It's not as much as my parents, but Susie and I can live well on it." He made another fist, which he smacked into his palm. "I should have told her that. I'm going to pack a bag and get on the next train. Did you say she was going to a town called Pueblo?"

"Yes, but no train goes through there. She was heading to Denver and then someone from the man's ranch was supposed to pick her up and take her to Pueblo."

"I'll get there as quick as possible. Take a train to Denver and then get a horse and ride to Pueblo."

"You know how to horseback ride, Mr. Kane?"

He nodded. "My parents have a friend outside the city who owns horses. Father always enjoyed riding. I leaned as a child. I'm a very good horseman, as a matter of fact. I assume whoever is meeting Susie would take a buggy and drive her."

Lottie nodded. "I guess so."

"A single horse is faster than a buggy. I can make good time. Maybe even get to Pueblo before she does."

"Mr. Kane, I wish you the best. I hope you find her."

He almost shouted his reply, "I will find her! I love Susie. I won't let her get away from me because of a misunderstanding."

"I know she loves you too, Mr. Kane. The only reason she left is she believed you would never marry her."

"She's wrong, and I'm going to prove that to her." He almost leaped up from his seat. "I have to go. I need to pack a suitcase, get to the train station, and find a map of Colorado. All I know about it is it's a state out West. I never thought I'd be traveling there."

"If there's anything I can do, just let me know."

"Thank you. There. I'm packing and going directly to the train station. There's no time to waste. If you could please tell my parents where I'm going I'd appreciate it."

"Of course."

Kane didn't walk. He ran to his residence and took three minutes to pack his suitcase. When he got to the train station, the clerk told him he was lucky. A train headed to Chicago was scheduled to leave in thirty minutes. In St. Louis, he could change trains and board one headed for Denver.

"A first-class ticket," Kane said.

"Yes, sir. The train doesn't seem to be full. Guess not that many people are headed out to Denver today."

"Good. I don't like crowds," Kane said.

The clerk handed him the ticket. "Have a good trip."

———————

Lucky felt silly standing at the train station holding a sign in his hands and waving it as passengers left the train. He felt silly and stupid. Every passenger looked at him like he was a dumb child. But he wasn't about to complain to Smiley or risk putting down the sign and miss connecting with Susie Thomas. The penalty for disobeying orders in the Smiley Gang could be a bullet.

He groaned when the thought hit him: What if Susie what's-her-name can't read? There were still a lot of people who couldn't. What could he tell Smiley? *Boss, the lady never showed up.* That might be the truth, but Smiley would still not be happy. And when Smiley wasn't happy he tended to shoot things.

He walked a short ways then turned and walked back. He wondered if this was the right train, but it had to be. Smiley had told him the woman listed this train and this time to arrive in Denver. Lucky, like Smiley, had his picture on wanted posters. Which is why he preferred being in a big city. There were a lot of people in cities, and chances were they didn't bother looking at wanted posters. In small towns, men often walked into the sheriff's office to glance at the posters. He shook his head. If this was the right train, then where was she?

"Excuse me, sir. I'm Susie Thomas."

He turned around and was stunned at how attractive the woman was. He almost—almost—let words slip from his mouth that were not appropriate for a young woman's ears. Even worse, those words would have raised suspicions in the woman. Smiley said speak politely and treat the lady nicely until they got back to Pueblo. He gave a big smile.

"Good to meet you. Mr. Malone apologizes. He had to go to Wyoming to meet with a cattle buyer. It was somewhat unexpected. So he asked me to come down and escort you to the ranch. My name is Lucky Lynn. I'm the foreman of his ranch, ma'am." Lucky prided himself that he could lay words on like molasses on pancakes if he needed to. Sunday-go-meeting words.

Susie smiled. "Thank you for meeting me. Is Pueblo a long way from here?"

"It will be a two-day journey, ma'am, with the buggy. Mr. Malone said don't take it too fast. We have some good-sized bumps in the roads around her. Mr. Malone was afraid I'd hit one and bounce you out of the buggy. He said if that happened, you'd want to go back to Philadelphia."

"That's very kind of Mr. Malone, but I think I can take a bump or two."

Lucky noticed the woman was carrying two suitcases. He tossed the sign away. "Here, ma'am. Let me take those, and I will show you to the buggy."

"Thank you. Two days, you said?"

"Yes, ma'am. But don't worry. We can reach Lattigo in a few hours and we can stop along the way to let you stretch your legs. Lattigo does have a good hotel. Mr. Malone has already made an arrangement for your room. You can get a good night's sleep after that long trip you took."

"Mr. Malone is very considerate."

You don't know the half of it, Lucky thought. He walked to the buggy, lifted the suitcases, and put them in back of the seat. He started toward the driver's seat then quickly halted. He gently touched Susie's elbow and escorted her to the passenger's side and helped her step up into the buggy.

Ought to get extra pay for this, he thought. On second thought, he knew exactly how the young lady could pay him back for being so nice to her. He stepped up into the driver's seat and grabbed the reins.

"I must admit, ma'am, my job doesn't usually entail driving buggies. I may not be too good at this."

"I trust you, Mr. Lynn. I'm sure you'll do fine."

You're gonna regret those words, lady, Lucky thought.

CHAPTER 5

Cully had tied his horse to the hitching post outside the sheriff's office in Pueblo and prepared to mosey inside. Cully thought he was good at moseying. He could be quick if he had to, and he could dodge bullets with the best of men. But walking or riding, he often struck a languid stride, as if he had no place to go and in no particular hurry not to get there. But as he was about to walk toward the door, a young man ran in front of him. Cully smiled at the impatience of the young, but then he frowned and narrowed his eyes.

The young man had looked worried, anxious. Not just an ordinary worry, either. The man looked like he was in anguish. Cully pulled his saddlebags from his mount and walked more slowly into the office. He couldn't help but overhear the conversation the man was having with Sheriff Virgil Hagin.

Hagin leaned back in his chair. "Are you telling me, Mr. Kane, that your fiancée was coming out here to be a mail-order bride?"

"Yes, sir. It was a huge misunderstanding. I want to marry the lady. I love her. She thought I never would, so she accepted an invitation to be a mail-order bride from a man named Luther Malone. He has a big ranch around here," Kane said.

"No, he doesn't," the sheriff said. "I'm sorry, Mr. Kane, but I've been sheriff here for eight years, and there's no one named Luther Malone lives here. There are a couple of large ranches, but the owners are not named Malone."

Kane looked like a pail of cold water had been poured over him. He shook his head. "That can't be. It... it can't be..."

Cully noticed the look of panic on the young man's face. He knew men who had advertised for mail-order brides and knew two who were happily married to their eastern wives. But he also knew some letters seeking mail-order brides were fraudulent. A despicable scheme, he thought, one of the most vile in the west.

"Son, maybe you better go back east. I'm guessing you've never been west of the Mississippi. It's a different world out here. Believe me, it's completely different from what you've experienced back there."

Kane slammed his fist on the sheriff's desk. "No! Susie is here, and I'm going to find her. I don't care how long it takes. I'll be here forever, if need be."

Cully stood silent, but he was impressed with the young man. Young love, he thought, was not always wise, but it was admirable. He sensed the young man did have courage.

"OK, stay here," the sheriff said. "You have a gun?"

The question caught Kane by surprise. "Er... no, I've never used a gun."

"If you're going to stay out here, I suggest you buy one, and then you need somebody to train you how to use it. You could ask Cully over there. He certainly knows how to use a gun. Or you might hire him to find your fiancée. He knows the West as good as he knows guns. He's here to collect a reward for bringing in an outlaw. I've got your money, Cully."

Cully smiled and walked over to the desk.

Sheriff Hagin reached in a drawer and drew out an envelope. He gave it to Cully. "A hundred dollars. Ainsley was one of the cheaper outlaws. He didn't have much of a bounty."

Cully tore open the envelope and counted the twenties. "A hundred is not bad for a day's work. He was wanted dead or alive. I would have brought him in alive, but he shot at me."

"And missed," Hagin said.

"Yes, in my profession you appreciate people with lousy aim."

Hagin pointed to Kane. "Young man, I'm sorry about your fiancée, but you would be utterly lost out here. You're likely to get yourself killed. If you're looking for someone, I suggest you hire Cully. He can find people, both honest people and criminals."

Cully nodded. "I might be able to give you some help, son."

"That's another trait of Mr. Cully here. He likes helping people. He's the white knight of the range. And I hear he doesn't charge all that much."

The anger seemed to flow out of Kane. He realized what the sheriff said was true. He had no knowledge of the West. He needed someone with knowledge of the area and someone who knew how to use a gun. "Mr. Cully, would you mind taking a few minutes and talking with me? I can pay you for your time."

"Well, let's not talk about money yet, son. Do you drink?"

"Yes, and right now I feel like I need one."

"Come over with me to the Prairie Dog Saloon. I'll buy the first round. You will need to tell me everything you know about your fiancée's trip to Colorado."

Five minutes later, the two sat at a small round table. Glasses holding whiskey sat in front of both. A bottle also sat on the table. Nervously, Kane sipped from the glass while providing Cully details of what had happened in Philadelphia. He sighed and drained his glass. Cully picked up the bottle and refilled Kane's glass.

"I should have told Susie earlier that I was going to ignore my parents' objections to the marriage. I didn't care what they said. But right now that doesn't matter. I just want to find Susie, take her back east, and marry her."

"Mr. Kane, I need a place to begin if I'm going to find your future bride. Did the letters give any details about this supposed ranch in Colorado? Are you sure it was in Pueblo?"

Kane nodded. "Yes. I didn't see the letters—I think there were two—but Susie shared them with her best friend, a girl named Lottie Raulerson. She said this Luther Malone had a ranch in Pueblo—a large ranch—and had promised her she would have a good life. Beyond that, there were not many details. I think Susie loves me, but she was distraught when she thought we couldn't get married. I mean, if she tells me to go home, I'll go home. But I really believe she'll want to come back with me as my wife."

"First, we have to find her," Cully said. He took a sip of his drink. "I need to ask you this again, because it's very important. From what Miss Raulerson told you, Pueblo was the only town mentioned in the letters? There was no other town or region in Mr. Malone's letters?"

"That's the only town Miss Raulerson said was mentioned. If that's the town Mr. Malone lives in, why should he mention any other place?"

"A good question," Cully said.

He didn't tell Kane that he suspected there was no rancher named Mr. Malone. The letter, Cully suspected, was a lure to get young women to come to the West. He didn't want to reveal his suspicions to Kane. The young man had enough to worry about.

"There's no Luther Malone in these parts, or Sheriff Hagin would know it. But perhaps the writer of the letter did reveal something by mentioning Pueblo. I will have a look around. You get a room at the hotel, and I will keep in touch."

"Mr. McCullough—"

"Call me Cully. Everybody does."

"Cully, I'm desperate. My family is well-off and I have money myself. I'll pay a thousand dollars to get Susie back."

"We won't worry about money now. The most important thing is getting Miss Thomas back to you although I wouldn't mind a thousand-dollar payday. It's late today. Get a hotel room and dinner. Tomorrow I will be roaming around. As I said, I will keep in touch."

When Kane left for the hotel, Cully walked back to the sheriff's office. He nodded to Sheriff Hagin after opening the door. "I saw something on your bulletin board this afternoon and wanted to check it out, if you don't mind."

"Not at all."

Cully walked over to where all the wanted posters were. About a dozen were pinned to the wall. He ran his fingers over them. He found the picture that he had caught a glimpse of earlier. Horace "Smiley" James. The charges against James included murder, bank robbery, a federal charge of robbery of a post office, and kidnapping. Cully's gaze lingered on the kidnapping charge.

"Sheriff, the reason you have a poster of Mr. James here—besides all the accusations—is that he has operated in this region, correct?"

Hagin nodded. "Yes, he was born not far from here. One of the murder charges against him is for killing a man up in Sykes Canyon, which is only about ten miles from here."

"So he still might be hanging around Pueblo?"

"Could be," the sheriff said.

CHAPTER 6

The next morning, Cully saddled Samson and climbed into the saddle. He had spent some of the night thinking about Sherman Kane and his lost fiancée. Cully didn't like the conclusions he was coming too. He softly spurred Samson. The horse trotted down the street. A couple of items, he thought, were clear.

One, the letter to young Susie Thomas of Philadelphia was phony. There was no Luther Malone in Pueblo or in any other city in Colorado. The writer did not want Miss Thomas for a wife, but for other, more nefarious purposes. Cully thought what the writer had planned for the young woman was a version of modern-day slavery, and it was despicable.

Two, he had to hope the mention of Pueblo was not just a name pulled out of the wind. He hoped the writer had actually named the town where his base of operations was. As Samson trotted toward the city limits, Cully knew he had to find it. But if he was right, the letter writer and his friends needed a house, a rather large house. It was possible to have such an establishment twenty miles out in the barrens. Possible but not likely. Such an establishment needed to be close to a town.

He roamed around the few streets in Pueblo but saw nothing to interest him. He headed south on the main road.

When he passed the two-story house a half-mile away, his eyes narrowed. He eased Samson toward it.

He tried to remember the history of the house. It had been built as a hotel years ago, but something had happened to the owner. He went bankrupt, or was shot, or broke his neck in an accident. But for whatever the reason, he disappeared and never returned.

The fact that it was originally meant as a hotel stuck in his mind. A hotel would be useful for what the phony letter writer had in mind. As Cully rode closer, he saw two men sitting outside. He guessed the house was fifty yards back from the road, on a small hill. He couldn't get a close look at them, but he didn't think they looked respectable from a distance. Cully doubted a closer view would change his mind.

Samson kept strolling by the house. Two stories, Cully thought. But he noticed something odd. On this side, it appeared there were six rooms on the second floor. The windows of four of the rooms were open. The light breeze blowing waved the curtains in the rooms. But in two rooms, the windows were shut and blinds covered the openings.

That was strange, he thought.

Samson trudged passed the hotel. "Think I need to check that out," Cully muttered to himself. Don't want to waste time, but tonight would be better than in the day.

———

"You notice that man?" Baxter said as he glanced at the road from the porch. "Had the eyes like a frog in a gully drencher. Like he could see things."

"Don't get nervous. He was just a cowpoke passing by," said Palmer.

"No, he wasn't. The guy looked at us like a mountain lion looking at his prey. Sneakily crawling up to it, ready to pounce."

"Baxter, go in and have a drink to steady your nerves. You are seeing things."

"I think we need to check him out. Maybe I'll follow him—"

"No, you won't!" Palmer said sharply. "You're gonna stay here on this porch and watch men ride by, or you're gonna stay in the house drinking. Smiley's orders were not to move until he gets back. He has planned this for a while, made his plan, and he doesn't want any deviations from it. You know how Smiley reacts when his orders are not obeyed."

Baxter was about to get out of his chair. After listening to Palmer's words he settled back down. "Wish he would get back."

"He'll be back when he gets here. Smiley is doing more planning or whatever. At times he tells us what he's doing, and other times he plays his cards close to his chest. He'll be back when he finishes. Until he gets here, we don't do anything besides drink and admire the scenery."

"Wish he'd change that rule about being the first to sample the ladies," Baxter said.

"You get that out of your mind. That's an ironclad rule. He's not going to change it, and if you even thinking about breaking it, we'll dig a plot for you behind back. But don't expect anyone to say any words over you. We ain't preachers."

Baxter shook his head. "Think I will get a drink." He rose from his chair and went into the house.

Several minutes later, Palmer was still in his seat when the stranger rode back toward town. Palmer studied the man for a moment. Tall, muscled. There was a strength about the man. The stranger didn't look toward him. A slight uneasiness flowed over Palmer. As an outlaw, Palmer felt he could sense a lawman a mile away, and he wondered if the stranger was wearing a badge. There was something about him. He shook his head. "Take your own advice and keep calm," he said aloud. "He's just a stranger riding a horse."

He watched as the stranger rode back to town. But... that was odd, Palmer thought. The man rides past the hotel, but just five minutes later he rides back? A few people ride out of Pueblo, but they don't generally ride right back in. Odd... but it was none of his business and had nothing to do with the hotel. He sighed and thought he might join Baxter in having a drink. He stood up. Lucky should be getting back tonight with the mail-order bride. Smiley didn't say when he would return, but it had to be soon.

He turned and walked into the house, taking one last glance at the tall stranger.

In the evening, the buckboard being driven by Lucky pulled up at the hotel. Two men came out to welcome him.

Susie, puzzled, felt traces of fear rise in her chest. She swallowed. A coldness gripped her stomach. "Mr. Lynn, what's going on? This isn't a ranch."

Lucky gave a wide but ugly smile. His face twisted into a menacing grimace. He reached up, grabbed her, and swung her off the seat. "No, little lady, it isn't. But it is your new home."

He grabbed her mouth before she could scream. He then grabbed her arms as Baxter pulled her legs from the ground.

"We'll take her to a room and tie her up. She'll be here with Smiley returns. That will make him happy," Lucky said. "Can you do your thing, Palmer?"

"Sure, it will be easy with this. Just one little tap and she's out." Palmer had killed one man by slamming his pistol butt against the man's head. But he could also use a lighter touch and knock men or women out using the butt of his gun. Besides a slight ache, there were no ill effects.

"Nothing more than a tap. We don't want her sick. We want her in prime shape."

"She'll be fine," Baxter said.

At about that time, Cully was in the hotel room of Sherman Kane, who looked weary. Cully sensed Kane was a man who went out in public finely dressed, with every hair in place. But tonight his hair was very much out of place. It looked like he had splashed water on his face and head from the basin in the room but hadn't combed his hair or wiped all the water droplets off his face.

Cully didn't sit down. "Mr. Kane, I need you to tell me what Miss Thomas looks like." For a moment, Cully wondered if the man understood him but finally Kane nodded.

"Susie is about five foot five, brown hair, not too long. It's cut short. She's slender but not thin. Gray eyes, which despite all she's been through, usually sparkled. She has a regular voice, not too high or too low. Usually there's some gaiety in it. I hope it's still there."

"It should be after tonight."

Kane's eyes widened in hope. "What do you mean?"

"I can't tell you yet, because I might be wrong. But I might have a clue about Miss Thomas's whereabouts. I'm going to check it out tonight."

Kane jumped from his chair. "I'll go with you! I can help!"

Cully held up his hand. "No, you can't!"

"But—"

Cully's voice was hard. "No buts! I know you want to help, but believe me, where I'm going you couldn't help. You would be more of a hindrance. You've never handled a gun, Kane. I'm going into a situation where that could get you killed—or get Miss Thomas killed.

"Besides, I work best alone. Frankly, I'm very good at working alone. So if I'm lucky and I'm right, I will need to work alone tonight. If I'm wrong, I keep searching." He saw the dejection on Kane's face and added, "There is something you can do."

"What? Anything!"

"This depends on how much money you have."

"I have enough, whatever it is. And I will spend every penny I have to get Susie back."

Cully nodded. "OK, the livery stable here has buggies for rent. About ten minutes before closing time, I want you to rent one. Drive it behind the hotel. Make sure the horses are fed and watered. I'm not going to promise anything, but as my father might have said, if God is with us I will have Miss Thomas back to you sometime tonight. When I do, you two get in the buggy and get out of here.

"About thirty miles northwest of here is a town called Castle Pines. There's a pretty good road to it. You get in the buggy and drive there. It's a bigger city than Pueblo, and there is a train depot there. Get a ticket back to Philadelphia and head out. There may be people trying to follow you, so get out as quickly as possible. You should get to the town well before morning, and if I'm not mistaken, trains going east stop there almost every day. By mid-day tomorrow you should be on your way back east."

Kane nodded. "Thank you. I—"

"Don't thank me yet. If I bring Miss Thomas to you tonight, you can shout thanks as you head for Castle Pines. But I might go out tonight and come back with nothing. That is a possibility, and you have to keep that in mind."

"I understand. Let me have your address. If Susie and I leave tonight, I'll cable you some money. I don't have a thousand on me right now."

"Don't worry about it. Our first job is getting you and Miss Thomas back to Philadelphia." Cully smiled. "You wouldn't have a bottle in the room, would you?"

"Yes, I do. I don't drink much, or I didn't before all this happened. Bought a bottle this morning. There may be only half a bottle left…"

"Then you've showed admirable restraint, Kane. Let's bring out the bottle and have one drink before we proceed. We both may need one."

Kane opened a drawer and pulled out the bottle of whiskey. He handed it to Cully. Cully pulled the cork out.

"Just one tonight. If all goes well, we can celebrate later."

———————

A half-moon showered the land with blue light as Cully rode to the hotel on the outskirts of town. The house was on an incline, but about a hundred yards away a deep ditch cut through the land. It was large enough to hide Cully's horse. He dismounted and his boots splashed in the water of the ditch. He peered over the bank.

Lights were on in the main room of the house. He could hear distant laughing. The upstairs was dark, but he remembered what rooms had the windows shut and blinds covering the openings. He raised his eyebrows when he saw the empty buggy in front of the house. The two horses had been unhitched and stood tied to a post at the side of the building.

The buggy meant someone had arrived late. He didn't think it was a man or, at least, only one man. A buggy was used to carry a woman, or possibly an ill man who couldn't ride a horse. But he didn't think the building had been changed into a medical office. Cully reasoned a woman had been brought in during the evening. Possibly the woman was Susie Thomas. But he was sure she wasn't staying at the locale voluntarily.

He planned to wait until the occupants went to bed. He hoped they were drinking, so they would sleep soundly when they finally went to bed. Then he would sneak into the building and get a firsthand look.

His hands tightened on his rifle. He almost wanted the men inside to try to stop him. They were in a despicable business. They should be shot or at least arrested and thrown in jail. But he would be content if they slept through the rescue and kept snoring while he rode with Miss Thomas to the town.

He was a good tracker, and he moved as quietly as any mountain lion in the forest or brush. He crept over the bank and moved as silently as the wind. He ran toward the house. He flattened on the ground when he thought he heard a sound. Tense and alert, he listened while lying flat. Only a cricket disrupted the silence. It was having a grand time chirping, but it was off-key. Cully raced up silently as he crept to the lit window. He paused and listened. He could hear the voices inside.

"How long will the young lady be out?"

"Early morning, Boss. She'll be groggy but nothing more," came the reply.

"Well, good. I will meet her tomorrow morning and welcome her to our establishment."

The statement was met with laughter. "Smiley, how many women you plan to get?"

Smiley. I was right, Cully thought. The head of the gang was Smiley James. Cully clenched his rifle. Smiley would not be smiling too much longer.

"I've got three letters out to women in the East. One has already said yes and expects to board the train this week for a trip to Denver and a life on the largest ranch in eastern Colorado."

"You promoted yourself. You only had a big ranch in the first letter. Now you're the owner of the biggest ranch in this part of the state."

"A man has to have ambition, boys."

More laughter. "Where did you learn how to write so sweetly, Boss?"

"In life you have to be tough, which we are, but sometimes you have to be sweet too. I learned that early. At times you get things done with a gun. But at times you can get a few things down with a smile. That's how I got the nickname Smiley. The key is knowing when to use a smile and when to use a gun."

Tonight if you get in my way, a gun is going to be used not a smile, Cully thought. He listened carefully. Three distinct voices came from the house. When he rode past the house earlier in the day, he saw two cowboys. Add in the buggy—that had to have a driver. That makes three men at the house.

But from the conversation, Smiley wasn't there when the woman was taken in. He had asked about the new woman. That meant another man had been driving the buggy. So there was at least one more outlaw in the house. Four. Perhaps one was not a big talker. As long as he was a big drinker, Cully thought.

Smiley was the one who had traveled back recently. Perhaps he'd be tired from the trip and would sleep deeply tonight. From the sounds beyond the window, Cully guessed the men were drinking while talking. He wanted them to keep drinking.

Cully thought for a moment. He didn't mind killing scum like the four men in the house, but he didn't want a confrontation tonight. If he could get in and get out quickly with no trouble, he could get Miss Thomas to her fiancé and off to Castle Pines without any trouble. Any gunplay and the outlaws might chase him and Miss Thomas to town… although that would be risky. They wanted to keep in the shadows and away from the local sheriff. Chasing a rider through town and shooting at him would tend to attract attention.

Even so… it would be better for Miss Thomas if there were no shots fired tonight. Assuming Miss Thomas was on the second floor. Cully told himself that was his theory, but it rested more on a hunch than concrete evidence. He had played hunches before and had been successful. But he had also experienced surprises in life. Maybe the gang just had illegal whiskey in the second-floor rooms. Or illegal whiskey and kidnapped women.

The conversation turned to prior criminal behavior, with the men noting a train robbery they had taken part in and a stagecoach robbery where a man had been killed.

"Those days are over, boys. As I said before, we're not going to go out and chase money anymore. It's going to come to us. Our customers are going to open their wallets and willingly hand us cash, and we won't even have to shoot them."

A roar of laughter came from all around. "That sounds better than our previous profession, Boss. No hard riding, no sleeping out on the prairie, no dodging sheriffs and posses."

"This job will be profitable but will have a lower risk." Smiley laughed. "We won't be shooting out customers, and they won't be shooting back at us."

They might not, but that doesn't mean I won't, Cully thought.

The night air was cool, but Cully didn't shiver. A friend had told him once that he seemed impervious to heat or cold. If he was tracking an outlaw, he focused on his job and nothing else. Now he focused on Smiley and his gang.

But he was still glad a few minutes later when he heard the outlaw leader say he had ridden many miles during the day and was going to get some sleep. He then made a crude remark about the "guests" in the house. Cully figured the outlaws would follow their leader and get some sleep. The conversations dimmed.

Cully waited for silence. When he didn't hear any talking for five minutes, he rose and peeked into the window. No outlaw remained in the room. A kerosene lantern burned low, casting some light in the room. He wondered if he should enter through the back door. But it might be locked. The outlaws hadn't locked the front door.

He waited for another ten minutes to make sure the gang was sleeping. He walked toward the porch and carefully eased up the steps. He reached for the door handle, pressed it, and pushed the door open. He crept toward the stairs, listening for any sound or movement.

Rifle in hand, he moved silently up the stairs, pausing when he reached the top. He knew where the two closed rooms were. If they had their captives tied up, which Cully suspected, there would be no reason to lock the door. But as he tried the knob, it wouldn't turn.

"That sours my milk," Cully muttered.

He tried again, but the handle didn't move. He stepped back from the door.

"Hope they're sleeping soundly," he said. He pounded his boot on the door, ripping the lock from the wood.

The door banged on the wall. He rushed in. Sitting on the bed was a woman who looked remarkably like Sherman Kane's description of his fiancée. She jumped off the bed, back against the wall.

"Don't worry. Sherman Kane set me," Cully said. Her eyes had looked groggy, but his words knocked the drowsiness from her face. He was glad she was awake. One of the outlaws had bragged about his ability to knock ladies out. He wasn't as good as he thought he was. Which was lucky for Cully.

"Sherman! How did he—"

"I'll explain later. Let's go!"

She moved toward him as he looked down the hall. Kicking the door off the hinges could have woken the sleeping outlaws. But at first he saw nothing. He felt Miss Thomas behind him.

"All right, let's not waste time. Run toward the stairs. I'll follow," he said. As she started into the corridor, Cully yanked her back.

At the end of the corridor, Jake Baxter ran from his room barefoot, pants on, but his shirt was his red underwear. He held a gun in his hand and spotted Cully at the door of one of the rooms. Baxter aimed, but Cully snapped his rifle up and fired. Two darker spots of red appeared on Baxter's chest. The bullets knocked him back against the wall. He opened his mouth, but no words out came out. His gun dropped to the floor. He hit the stair railing and pitched over, groaning as he fell to the first floor.

"Go!" Cully yelled.

Susie ran toward the stairs. Cully ran after her. As they turned to start down the stairs, a bullet ripped into the wood beside his head. He turned quickly and fired, spaying his bullets across the hall.

Lucky had been running toward him. But luck had run out for Lucky. One of Cully's bullets caught him in the heart. He staggered and fell head first onto the floor.

Other yells came from the rooms. Susie ran down the stairs but slipped and fell on the railing. She grabbed it to keep herself from falling. As he ran down the stairs, Cully grabbed her and kept running. When he reached the first floor, he turned swiftly, rifle ready.

Mudsy stood at the top of the stairs. He fired his pistol at Cully. But he had not sobered up from the night's drinking. The bullets flew two inches over Cully's head. Mudsy's legs were unsteady as he fired again. But the bullet sailed wide again.

"Can't miss that big a target," Cully said as he aimed and fired again.

His words proved true. Two bullets crashed into Mudsy's flesh. Mudsy tried to bring his hand to his stomach to cover the wound. He groaned and wobbled on his unsteady legs. Weakened by the bullets, he tipped forward and fell, tumbling down the stairs.

With his hand around Susie's waist Cully half ran, half stumbled outside and headed for his horse. He looked back but saw no one running after them... yet.

When they got to Samson, Cully picked Susie up and planted her in the saddle. He jumped up behind her and spurred Samson toward town. As they rode, Cully heard shots in the background, but the bullets plumped harmlessly in the sand.

Samson galloped into Pueblo. Cully turned him into the alley behind the hotel. In a second, he spied Kane standing beside the buggy. He halted Samson and lifted Susie from the saddle.

"Susie!" Kane yelled. He ran toward her and hugged her.

"Sorry, there's no time for long hellos. Get into the carriage. Kane, get into the driver's seat."

As Kane climbed into the buggy, Cully lifted Susie and laid her in the back.

She grabbed his arm. "I must tell you something. There's another woman up there," Susie said.

"What?"

"I heard her in the next room. I heard men going in, bringing her food. They said a few words, and I think she said a few words. I could barely make it out. But I heard someone walking around in that room."

"Thanks for telling me. I was planning a return trip, anyway. Their outlaw days will soon be over."

Susie eased back down in the buggy.

"She might be a little dizzy for a while, Kane. Don't worry. The outlaws knocked her out but didn't want to harm her. She'll be fine."

"Thank you, Cully. I've got your address. I'll send your money."

Cully smiled. "Kane, I'm sure you will. You're an honorable man. Don't stop until you get to Castle Pines. Then go back to Philadelphia and be happy."

Kane flicked the reins. The horses trotted toward the street.

The two outlaws, not fully clothed, stood outside the house.

"Who was that?" Smiley said. He wasn't smiling.

"I know that guy, Boss," Palmer said. "I caught a glimpse of him earlier today. I just realized I've seen him before. He's a guy named Cully. Bounty hunter at times. Lawman other times."

Smiley looked him. "You sure?"

Palmer nodded. "I'm sure. It's been two years since I've seen Cully. But believe me, Boss, once you've seen Cully in action, you don't forget him. Ever."

Smiley spit on the ground. "Then all those people who remember him can attend his funeral. Because we're going to kill him."

CHAPTER 7

Palmer slid the scrambled eggs onto the plate that already held three sizzling strips of bacon. He took the plate in one hand and grabbed the coffeepot with the other. He set the plate down before a scowling Smiley James and poured coffee in his cup.

"The only good thing about last night is that varmint sure ain't a yellow belly. Came in here, killed three of us and walked out alive," Smiley said. His voice was low, almost a growl.

"Yes, Boss."

"We're gonna need more men, and I'm gonna get them today. I know where I can hire a few."

Palmer set the coffeepot back on the stove. "If you don't mind my saying so, Boss, are you sure we shouldn't pack this in? Cully is bound to tell the sheriff, then we'll have the law sticking their necks into our business. We got three dead. If you believe in signs—"

"I don't!" Smiley said. He drank some of his coffee then lifted his pistol from his holster. "I believe in this. I believe in bullets and lead. I believe in leaving my enemies pushing up daises under a cement slab with the date of their death on it."

"You don't think this scheme is, well… collapsing. With Cully—"

"I'm going to take care of Cully. Soon he won't give us any more trouble." The tone became even more menacing. "This plan is going to work. I've been thinking about this for years, putting it together, figuring it out. We can keep stealing and riding hard forever. In our old business, sooner or later a sheriff's bullet would plug us. I planned this for a long time, and I'm not going to let it slip out of my fingers!" He emphasized the words by slamming his fist on the table. It shook so much, some eggs slid over the plate and onto the wood. "As for Cully, soon they'll be shoveling dirt on him."

———————

As the train rolled across the tracks headed for St. Louis, Susie kept hugging Kane. She didn't want to be separated from him, even by an inch. She knew how close she had come to an almost unimaginable fate. Whenever she thought of the house just outside the town limits of Pueblo, a coldness grabbed her stomach, and ice seemed to halt the flood of blood in her veins.

"It's all right, Susie. You're safe now," Kane told her. Her arm was around her shoulders. "You're safe now. We're fifty miles from Pueblo now, and we won't make a stop until we're fifty more."

"You sure they can't catch us?"

"A horse can't catch a train, honey. A good horse might match it in a sprint, but not for two miles much less fifty miles. The outlaws who kidnapped you are way behind us. That is, if there are any outlaws left, after Cully got through with them."

She breathed a sigh of relief. "I think he shot at least two. I mean, everything was so rushed it seems like a dream, a nightmare. But I think I saw two men go down."

"I'm sure you did. We're safe. We'll be in St. Louis soon, and then we have to change trains to get to Philadelphia. But in two or three days, we'll be home, and soon after that, we'll be married and starting a new life."

'I'm so glad you ran into Mr. Cully. He's a real nice man," Susie said.

"Yes, he is. I need to send him some money too. A thousand dollars."

"A thousand?"

"Yes, that's what I told him I'd pay him if he could find you," Kane said.

"A thousand? You put a high value on my life."

"You're worth that and more, honey. I would have pay ten thousand to get you back."

"That's so wonderful, Sherman. And... I thought you'd never marry me because of your parents."

"My parents are old-fashioned, but they've been good parents. There are times when a man has to make a stand, and I know we were meant for one another. My parents can accept that, or they can forget about seeing any of their grandchildren." He took a deep breath. "But I think when things settle down, they will accept you, then begin to like you, and then love you, because they will finally see what a wonderful woman you are."

She leaned her head on his shoulder. "That sounds wonderful. It will be a wonderful life."

"Yes, it will."

"And we should invite Mr. Cully to the wedding."

Kane nodded. "We can. I would enjoy seeing him again. But I'm not sure he will accept. I think Mr. Cully is a man of the West, of the open plains and the valleys. I have a feeling he doesn't like cities and doesn't like to be in one."

"But he won't be in one for long. Just time enough for the wedding, and then he can head back West."

Kane nodded. "Maybe he will attend. I'll tell him I'll pay him a bonus if he joins us at the church."

"I think you should. But I'm feeling guilty. You're spending a lot of money on me. You're not going bankrupt, are you?"

Kane laughed, titling his head as the laughter rolled out of him. "Don't worry about that," he told Susie. "I told you my parents have some good traits. One of my father's is the ability to make money. Bless his heart, father has a gift for business. He could take risks that no other businessman would and make them pay off—or stay away from an investment which looked good but later went bankrupt." He patted Susie's hand. "Some people have a keen sense of smell. They can smell violets from dandelions. They can tell the ingredients of a stew with one whiff. My father could smell out a good deal and detect the savory tinges of a bad deal. I don't know how he did it but he did it.

"One thing I do know is my father would go in his study and sit at his desk and think about a business proposal. And think and think. Might smoke a cigar, might read the Psalms. But he wouldn't come out until he had made a decision. And I don't think my father ever lost money on any business decision he made." He grinned. "Which makes it easier to put up with him when he has a blind spot, such as not wanting me to marry you."

Susie gave him a heartwarming smile. She liked how much he admired his father.

"But he'll come around. So don't worry about money. My father is also generous. Even if we disagree, I don't think he'd ever cut me out of his will, but even if he did, he has already been generous with me, and my bank account is doing fine."

"Good. I hated to think I was costing you a lot of money."

"You aren't. You haven't cost me anything. Knowing you has given me happiness, which is worth a lot more than money."

She smiled and laid her head on his shoulder.

––––––––––

Smiley stuck his boot in the stirrup and lifted himself onto his horse's back. Today, Smiley wasn't smiling. He had a deep frown on his face. He hadn't shaved, and the black stubble stuck out like cactus spines, giving him an angry, menacing look. Palmer stood on the porch.

"You sure about this, Boss? Maybe we should just pack up and leave. We've been riding together for three years and never got three men shot in any one night. There are times when you should pick up your losses and leave," Palmer said.

Smiley's reply sounded more like an animal's growl than a human voice. "No! No! No! I'm not going to let some polecat of a cowboy rob me of my dream. This is a good plan. It will make us rich. I told you all, we'd kill anyone who stood in our way, and I mean it. Now a man called Cully is in our way, and I will gut him and put him in his grave. I'm going now to get the men who will help me do it. Just stay here and take care of things."

Palmer nodded.

"If you need to contact me, send a telegram to Durango. That's where I'm going. I know some men down there who are for hire. I'll bring them up, and we'll start over. I know three or four men who are good with guns and don't care what type of work they're doing, as long as they get paid. The first thing we'll do when I get back is kill Cully. Then everything will be fine. Sorry we lost that cute little brunette from the east, but we'll replace her with other women."

"OK, if that's what you want, Boss. I'll also bury our friends. Got three bodies here in the house."

"Bury them deep. I ain't going to say words over them. I'm not a preacher. They were good men, but they knew the risks of the job. They should've been faster and better. There's no room for sentiment in this profession. You know any good men I might hire?"

"One or two. Dan Ballows over in Destin is usually available for hire. He's fast, and he doesn't miss. Last I heard, Ringo Starke was looking for a job. He can match Ballows in drawing a gun, and he shoots just as straight."

"Telegram them. Tell them if they want a job, I'm hiring. I'll pay a hundred dollars upfront if they join me. If they arrive here, tell them they're to kill a man."

"That won't bother them. And I already sent the telegrams. Got up early this morning. Figured you'd want them to come by. They're probably already in the saddle and headed this way."

"Good. Sounds like just the type of men I need. I'll be back in a couple of days. I'm gonna ride hard and fast."

Palmer waved goodbye. Smiley spurred his horse and galloped down the road.

———————

From the creek bed, Cully watched Smiley fade from sight as he rode toward Durango. A minute later, he saw Palmer open the door and go back into the house.

"He shouldn't be any problem," he said aloud. "But I never underestimate opponents. You always have to account for a lucky shot or an unlucky break. But there's still a young woman in that house, and I plan to get her out. If I can do it without killing a man, fine. But if I have to kill him, it's his own fault. But I will pay for his funeral. Don't want to cost the taxpayers any money."

CHAPTER 8

Palmer opened a bottle and eased down on a chair. He looked toward a room at the back of the house, the room where the three dead bodies had been stacked. He knew he was going to have an afternoon of work digging holes and dropping the bodies into them. He poured whiskey into a glass.

He wasn't going to curve three crosses. That was a waste of time. His outlaw buddies were not religious. They wouldn't care if a cross were at the head of their grave.

Three graves… that was a lot of work. He wondered if any of the three men would dig him a grave. He sipped the whiskey. Perhaps just one grave would be fine. He could toss all the dead gang members into one grave, fill it in, and be done with it. It would save him some time and prevent some aching muscles. He sipped some more whiskey and nodded.

"Lucky and the others won't mind that," he said aloud. "They were together for a while on the Earth. They can be together in eternity. One grave."

He grimaced when he realized he would not only have to dig the grave but lug the three men out to it. All three men were about his size. They would not be easy to carry.

"The dumb scalawags," he said. "At least one of them should have been able to shoot that dang Cully. He'd be alive and could help me carry the other two to their graves."

He drained the glass and poured one more drink. One more and then he would begin the task of saying farewell to his three fellow outlaws. He looked up toward the second floor. He drank the second glass of whiskey and headed for the stairs. He went up and unlocked the one bolted door on the second floor. The woman lay tied to the bed. He took off his gun belt and hung it on a chair. He undid the gag and sat the woman up. A mixture of surprise and fear came over her face.

"What are you doing?" she said. Her eyes became wide with fear.

He untied her hands. "I thought we should get to know one another a little better."

"I don't want to get to know you better."

"You should. I can make things easier for you. Would you like a drink?"

She shook her head vigorously.

"Smiley has laid down strict rules about enjoying our guests, but with all that has gone on, I don't think he would mind if I had a taste."

The woman drew back. "I heard shooting last night. What happened?"

"Three of my friends are dead. But it's no concern of yours."

He forced the woman back on the bed. "And we're going to kill the man who killed our friends."

A gruff voice came from the doorway. "That's going to be difficult, since you don't have a gun."

Palmer jumped up and spun around, and when he did, he stared into the business end of Cully's rifle.

"You were going to do what to me?"

Palmer didn't reply. He swallowed hard and coughed.

"You were talking mighty nice to the lady here," Cully said, walking toward him. "Tongue must have got stuck on the roof of your mouth. I'll help you with that."

He swung the butt of his rifle against Palmer's jar. The man groaned and tumbled to the floor. Once hit, he didn't move. Cully looked at the woman.

"Don't worry. I'm here to rescue you. I'm the guy who did the shooting last night."

For the first time in days her lips edged back in a small smile. "You?"

"Yes, ma'am. They talk hard and dirty, but they don't shoot too well. Three of them are dead." He pointed his rifle at Palmer. "Probably should have shot the guy on the floor, but I'm feeling charitable today. Never could shoot an unarmed man even if he's a rat. What's your name, ma'am?"

"Molly. Molly Bevins. I was in Northfield last I remember. Next thing I knew I was here tired up."

"They hurt you?"

"No. They brought me food three times a day but kept me tied up and gagged the rest of the time."

"I'll take you to town and get you into a real hotel."

He sat his rifle down and walked to Palmer. He searched the outlaw and pulled out some cash from his pocket. Cully counted seventy dollars. He gave it to Molly.

"You deserve this for all the trouble they caused you. Put that in your purse. It will buy you a first-class ticket back to Northfield and a lot more."

"Thank you... he... he mentioned a Cully. Is that you?"

"Yes. There was another lady they had kidnapped too. I got her out last night. I didn't know there was a second woman until she told me. That's why I came back."

'Thank you, again... I thought my life was over. And I was wishing that I could die.'

"Don't have to wish for that now. Your life will be much longer than that of the men who kidnapped you. You can go back to your home and have a happy life."

She pointed at Palmer. "What are you going to do with him?"

"Leave him on the floor. He'll wake up with a bad headache. Maybe that will teach him a lesson. Come with me. I'll escort you to town and to the stagecoach office. And perhaps we should stop in and have a long talk with the sheriff." He paused. "Come to think of it. I want to be there when this scum wakes. I want to ask questions about a man named Smiley. He's the leader of this gang."

"He's going to Durango," Molly said.

"What?"

"I heard them talking outside. They gagged me but didn't cover my ears. This guy was talking with another man this morning. The other man said he'd ride to Durango today. Said he knew men over there who would become part of the gang. Said they rode hard and killed easy. And they would kill you."

Cully smiled. "Is that so?"

She nodded.

"Well, killing me isn't going to be as easy as they think it. In fact..." He rubbed his chin. "I think I changed my mind. Think I will handle this a little differently than I first thought.

Anybody who will work for Smiley should be put out of action. The sheriff would probably like to hear about this. Would you do me a favor?"

"Certainly. You saved my life. Whatever you want, I'll do it."

"I'm going to drag this polecat in to the sheriff's office. If I do, would you identify him as one of the men who kidnapped you?"

"Sure, as long as he's behind bars."

Cully smiled. "Well, either he will be behind bars, or I'll be covering the varmint with my pistol. Either way, he won't touch you. What did you say his name was?"

"Palmer. Jasper Palmer." She sighed. "I'd like to have a bath and a good night's sleep. It's not sleeping when you are tied up. You don't feel like you rested any. Mind if I stay in town and get the stage tomorrow?"

"That will be fine. In fact, it will be perfect. Let's move, though. We'll get you into a hotel, and then I'll knock on the door when you need to identify Palmer. That's part one of the plan."

"Just don't get killed, Cully. I'm beginning to like you."

"I won't. That's not part of the plan."

Palmer was still passed out on the floor. Cully hauled him up and lifted him over his shoulder. Palmer, unconscious, said nothing. Cully carried him outside, tied his hands, and slung him over Samson.

"This won't take long. I'm tossing him into a jail cell, and then I'll come back."

Molly shook her head. "No! I don't want to be left here alone again. I'll walk with you."

Cully nodded. "That will be fine."

————————

After getting Molly a room at the local hotel, Cully dragged the still sleeping Palmer into the jail. He recounted his story to Sheriff Hagin and told him of his plan.

"Sounds sensible. But you won't even have to bother the young lady again. I think we can get Palmer's cooperation without having her come in," Hagin said.

As Cully followed him, Hagin found a bucket then walked outside and filled it halfway with water from a horse trough. When they walked back in, he handed the bucket to Cully while he opened the cell holding Palmer.

"You knocked him cold, Cully."

"Sometimes you get to enjoy your work."

With the door open, Hagin grabbed the bucket again and splashed water on Palmer.

The man yelped, sat up, and coughed. Water dripped from his face. His shirt and hair were soaked. "What the"

"Waking you up, Palmer. I'm Sheriff Hagin, and I want to talk to you."

Palmer's eyes appeared dazed. Then he saw Cully behind the sheriff and stiffened.

"Hello again," Cully said.

Palmer looked around realized he was in a jail cell. "Hey, what am I doing here? I didn't do anything."

Hagin smiled and spoke slowly, with confidence in his voice. "Yes, you did. A few minutes ago, while you were sleeping, we had a young lady come in and identify you as one of the men who kidnapped her and kept her prisoner for a few days. Said the man who did it was an ugly little varmint. So we figured that must be you. And it was. She identified you. Kidnapping is a serious offense. You could get twenty years for that. Twenty years of hard labor."

Palmer said nothing. Just directed a bitter stare at the sheriff and Cully.

"In addition to the young lady's testimony, I have the statement of Mr. Cully here that you were one of the outlaws that he traded bullets with last night to rescue another young lady, and you were at that house this morning and had Molly all tied up. So we have two witnesses," Hagin said. "We've got a tough judge here in Pueblo. Judge Harold Benedict. He might give you fifty lashes in addition to the twenty years. But maybe I can mitigate the sentence. Oh, perhaps you don't know what mitigate means. It means to lessen, get you a reduced sentence."

Palmer shook the water from his face. "Could I get a drink of whiskey in here?"

"Usually I'd say no, but in your case, if you get a bit talkative, I might give you a drink before we lock the door again. But to get it you will need to tell me everything you know about Smiley and what he was planning. You understand?"

Palmer nodded. "I understand."

"I'm glad about that. Now things should go very smoothly. I'm guessing Smiley and the rest of your gang were going to open a house of ill repute in this fine city. That is, until Mr. Cully came along. I understand that bushwhacker Smiley rode out this morning. Tell us where he's going, when he'll be back, and what his plan is. If you do, you get a drink of whiskey, and the judge might be lenient on you."

Palmer sighed. He brought his hand up and rubbed his head. "Smiley headed to Durango this morning. He said he could find gunmen there. Asked me if I knew anyone for hire. Told him about two men I thought was looking for work, Dan Ballows and Ringo Starke. They're over in Destin. Sent telegrams to them telling them if they needed work, we were paying top dollar."

Hagin thought for a moment. "Ballows. Starke. Those names are familiar. Bet I have some posters on them."

"I know Starke is wanted, but I'm not sure about Ballows."

"You tell them to come to the hotel?"

"Yes, told them I'd be there."

Hagin chuckled. "Well, you won't be, but a few other people will. You said Smiley wanted to hire a few more guns. How many men did he expect to pick up in Durango?"

"Three or four. We still had some money left from the robberies we pulled. He was going to give them a bonus upfront to get them to ride with us."

"Is there anything else we should know?" Hagin said.

"Smiley said if I needed to get in touch with him to send a telegram to Durango. Said he would telegram me if he needed me to do something."

"Is that so?" Cully said. "That's good to know." He looked at the sheriff. "We might be able to use that piece of information."

Palmer looked around. A trace of fear came into his eyes. "Hope you have plenty of deputies, sheriff. When Smiley learns I talked, he'll kill me."

"You don't have to worry about that. Mr. Smiley is going to have his hands full, won't he, Cully?"

"He'll have his hands and feet full, for that matter. He'll be dodging bullets, but he won't be able to dodge the rope we'll have ready for him."

"How about that drink?"

Hagin chuckled again, walked out of the cell, and slammed the door shut. In a minute he walked back and handed a glass of whiskey to Palmer. "Enjoy it. May be your last one for a long time."

Palmer took the glass, raised it to his lips and drained the glass. "Thank you, Sheriff," he said and handed the glass back.

Sheriff Hagin then went through the wanted posters, and he saw the name Ringo Starke. Starke had slick hair and a mustache. He was wanted for murder and bank robbery. His friend Dan Ballows was also wanted for murder, on two counts, along with a few lesser felonies. Hagin held up the posters. "Palmer knows the best people. These two guys are scum," he said.

"I didn't really expect him to hang around in high society," Cully said. "Destin is about two days' ride from here. So tomorrow they should be here, and they will go to the house. I'll be waiting for them."

"I could loan a deputy to you."

"No, I don't think that's necessary. Frankly, he'd just get in my way. However, I wouldn't mind if you deputize me. That means I'm legal."

"Sure I can do that. But you sure you don't want some help?" He tapped the posters with his finger. "These two have killed before."

Cully smiled. His deep voice didn't seem alarmed at all. "They weren't shooting at me. They're overdue at the cemetery. I'm going to see they get there."

"OK, if you say so." Hagin opened his desk and brought out a badge. "Raise your right hand."

Cully did so.

"Do you, Samuel McCullough, swear to uphold all the laws of the state of Colorado and the city of Pueblo, so help you God?"

"I do."

"Then you are officially a deputy of the town of Pueblo, for as long as you want the job."

"Thank you, Sheriff."

"So, Cully, what is the next step of this plan?"

Cully pinned the badge to his shirt. "Well, I thought I'd head to the house and welcome Mr. Barrows and Mr. Starke to town. After a brief discussion, I'll escort them down here to the jail. That's after I send Smiley a telegram telling him that the guy, Cully, broke into the house and stole the young lady."

"Why would you do that?"

"I want him angry, so angry he'll make mistakes. Even in tight situations, I've always managed to stay calm. A veteran Texas Ranger gave me a piece of valuable advice some years back, and it saved my life more than once. He told me, 'Never get angry. Keep your emotions under control. If you don't, you'll get angry and kill someone you didn't intend to kill or make a mistake and get killed yourself.' He was absolutely right. A tracker has to move by experience, intelligence, and instinct at times. Anger will disrupt or override all three. You have to keep calm."

"So you want to rile up Smiley."

"Yep. If I get him hissing like an angry rattler, he'll make mistakes. Even if he doesn't, I would just enjoy seeing him fume and yell like someone who got in the way of a skunk."

"I imagine he's going to be fuming so much that smoke will blow out of his ears," Hagin said. "Usually I prefer hanging outlaws, but I wouldn't mind if Smiley takes a bullet. Just so long as he's in the ground and not bothering anyone."

"Sheriff, by the way, do you know who actually owns the hotel that Smiley took over? Did he buy it? Or just walk in because it was abandoned?"

"To be honest, I don't know. I know it's been empty for some time. He might have been able to pick it up. If the owner up and leaves a building or property, then after the legal amount of time, any potential buyer can often purchase it for a minimal amount. Pays the back taxes on it, and it's his. I could check on that for you at the land office if you like."

Cully nodded. "I would, if you don't mind. Right now I'm going to go get some lunch. It's been a busy morning."

"If you need anything, just let me know."

"I'll do that, Sheriff. Usually I work alone, but it's nice to know I have men who will stand by me if needed."

CHAPTER 9

As he walked outside he whistled. He kept whistling as he strolled to the telegraph office. He smiled as he walked by men on the street and tipped his hat when he passed a woman. A calmness settled on him. Cully knew there was a mild contradiction in his personality, and he wondered about it from time to time. He was not a violent person. He would be content if he never fired another shot in anger, or fired another shot as a U.S. Marshal. He would fish, hunt, enjoy the wide-open spaces in the West and generally have a fine time. But he also knew he enjoyed—to a degree—times of danger, the times when he walked on the edge of life and death. He didn't seek them out, but it seemed to him the nearness and possibility of death gave him an ecstatic appreciation of life. That appreciation of life was strongest during the times he was dodging bullets. And at those times of danger, every nerve seemed alert. His vision seemed to improve. Hearing was sharpened. But at the same time that calmness always overtook him. He never panicked. He stayed calm even in the midst of ecstasy and danger.

He shrugged. That might be the life of every lawman.

When he walked into the telegraph office. It was empty of customers. The telegraph operated waved at him and said hello. "What can I do for you?" he asked.

"Like to send a telegram."

"That's what we do here."

The operator was a short, stout fellow who was balding. But he wore a happy smile and had a gaiety in his voice, as if was enjoying the day, his work, and life itself. He sat down behind his desk and grabbed a pencil. "Where do you want to send it?"

"Durango."

"Durango? That's not too far. Who are you sending it to?"

"A man named Smiley James."

The operator laughed. "Smiley. Now there's a name for you. I guess he must smile a lot."

"Not lately," Cully said. He didn't add that he didn't think Smiley would be grinning much in the upcoming days either.

"What would you like to say?"

"Say, 'Cully left with our guest. Said you are an outlaw and a coward. Said he will bring you back to Pueblo, so he can see you dangling at the end of a rope. Said he will pay two dollars for your funeral because he doesn't want to burden the taxpayers."

The operator widened his eyes and his hands shook as he wrote down the words. "Mister, are you—"

"Am I sure I want to say that? Yes. It should get his attention."

The operator nodded. "That's the truth." He moved to the telegram and began tapping the key. "Don't get many messages like this one," he said.

"I'm sure you don't." Cully listened until the tapping stopped. "How much do I owe you?" he said.

"Fifty cents will do it."

Cully handed over the money. He then reached into his pocket and brought out a ten-dollar bill. "One more thing. If you get a telegraph back from Durango addressed to a Jasper Palmer, let me know. He's in the jail, so I'm reading all his mail."

"I'll let you know," the operator said as he grabbed the money.

"Thank you. You do good work."

———————

Cully sipped his beer as the waiter eased the plate of roast beef, potatoes, gravy, and yellow corn in front of him. He had had a busy morning and, while leaving the telegraph office, realized he was very hungry. He picked up a knife and fork and cut the roast beef, then swallowed a slice. Delicious. The roast beef was tender, and the gravy was thick and tasty.

That was one problem in spending time in the plains or mountains. You had to eat your own cooking, and a campfire didn't make the best stove. He enjoyed the outdoors, and when he was in the wild, he felt close to the divine. But to get good food you needed a kitchen not just a campfire.

After the beef, he sampled the corn and potatoes, then smiled with satisfaction. You couldn't get food this good from a campfire. Cully also admitted that while he thought he had many talents, cooking wasn't among them. He just didn't have the knack.

He stabbed a second slice of beef. As he chewed, he thought there was an advantage to living in a town. Towns had restaurants, and you could always get a good meal. If he could only bring those restaurants with him into the mountains. He swallowed and thought the roast beef was some of the finest he had ever eaten. He signaled to the waiter as the man walked by. "My compliments to the cook. This is an excellent meal."

"I'll tell him, sir."

He was halfway through the potatoes and corn and more than halfway through the roast beef when a man approached the table. He was tall, thin and appeared a bit skittish. "Excuse me, are you Mr. Cully?"

"Ever since I was born. What can I do for you?"

"I'm Henry Dailey, Mr. Cully. I'm a teller at the bank. Mr. Emlet, the bank president, asked me to find you and tell you that a considerable amount of money has been wired to you."

"Really?"

"Yes, sir. A thousand dollars."

Cully smiled. "I see Mr. Kane is a man of his word. But I didn't expect payment this quickly."

"You can open an account at the bank, or we can give you the money in cash. First, I went to the sheriff. I was told you knew him, and he said you might be having lunch here. When you're through, if you could drop over to the bank..."

"I'll do that. Thank you, Mr. Dailey. Give me about fifteen minutes, and I'll visit your fine establishment."

Sherman Kane certainly was a man of his word, Cully thought. Cully had an appreciation for money but wasn't greedy for it. The first thought in his mind was to get a hotel room and take a week off. He could relax and eat in the restaurant for a week with more than enough money to pay the bills.

After he took care of Smiley and his gang.

———————

Ten minutes later he walked to the bank and into the office of Mr. Emlet, who was a bit taller but just as chubby and balding as the telegraph operator. Emlet stood up and walked around the desk to greet him, offering his hand. Cully shook it.

"Wanted to find you, Mr. Cully, before you left town, if you were still in town. We weren't sure at first, but the sheriff said you were here."

"I am indeed. Thanks for being so diligent."

"I think Mr. Dailey explained that you can open an account where we can deposit the funds, or we can give you the cash."

"Think I'll do both. I'll take about two hundred dollars and open an account with the rest."

"Certainly." He looked outside the door and waved to his employee. "Mr. Dailey, please open an account for Mr. Cully, and put eight hundred dollars in. Bring the remaining cash in here."

"Yes, sir."

"We're very glad to have your business, Mr. Cully."

"I'm glad I have enough money to do business with you, Mr. Emlet. Gives a man a sense of security to have an ample bank account."

"That's what we do. We provide people security."

Dailey knocked on the door then entered holding a wad of cash. He gave the money to Cully. "Here's your two hundred dollars."

"Thank you. Sorry I can't stay, gentlemen, but I need to go over to the funeral parlor and give the owner a little money."

Emlet looked puzzled. "The funeral parlor?"

Cully smiled. "Yes, there's going to be some funerals soon."

————

When Smiley read the telegram at the Durango telegraph office, he shouted curses about Cully, his family, and all of his ancestors. He quickly ran out onto the street and cursed some more. He ripped the telegram into a hundred small pieces and left them in the dirt after stamping on them a few times. His heel mashed some tiny bits of paper into the dirt. He gritted his teeth as he walked down the street. He wanted to yell some more, but he didn't want to attract the attention of the sheriff.

Cully would pay for what he did, Smiley thought. He would pay in blood. How in the world did he get involved? Nobody knew the first woman. And nobody knew the second one. She was two thousand miles away, from Philadelphia. No one could have come looking for her. Besides, Cully wasn't from the East. He knew that without even seeing the man. Cully was a Westerner. But how did he know about Susie Thomas?

Smiley shook his head. It didn't matter. Cully would be dead soon. But the man had cost him some money. He needed gunmen, and he would have to pay them and pay them well. But he still had money from the gang's holdups and robberies. He would spend every cent of it to make sure Cully died a painful death.

He walked into the saloon and demanded a bottle. He took it and sat down at a small table in the back. He was expecting company. He took two glasses with him. He poured whiskey in one and set the other on the table. It was for his first guest.

CHAPTER 10

Ten minutes later, a large man with a red beard on his pale face walked up. He must have weighed two hundred and fifty pounds, but there didn't appear to be any fat on him. His clothes were dusty, and mud was on his boots. But his gun belt looked clean, and his pistol had not even a speck of dust.

"You Smiley?" he said.

"I am. Sit down." Smiley reached for the bottle and poured his visitor a drink.

"You looking for men?"

"I am. Men who are good with guns."

"I'm very good with guns."

"I need you to help kill a man. Would that bother you?"

"Not if I get paid for it."

"Then sit down and let's talk. What's your name?"

"Deke Lomax," the red-bearded man said as he sat down in a chair. He lifted the glass and sipped the whiskey. "But killing a man is expensive, and I don't work cheap. How much are you offering?"

"For now, two hundred dollars, with fifty upfront and the rest when we kill a man called Cully. I won't lie to you. Cully knows how to use a gun. He's probably been a lawman, but I don't know for sure."

Lomax didn't seem bothered by Cully, but his lips widened into a big smile when he heard the pay Smiley was offering. "Two hundred?"

"Yes."

"You must really want him dead."

"I do. Cully interfered with a business I have over in Pueblo. It's a business that could become very profitable. If you want to stick around and be a guard for me, you'd probably easily make two hundred a month. You interested?"

"First things, first. I may or may not help you with the business, but I'll kill Cully for you.

"You'll have help. I'm hiring at least four men to help me get rid of him. If one or two want to stay around and help me with business that's fine."

"Four men. You must think there's safety in numbers."

"Let's just say I'm not overconfident. If four men ride out against Cully, less than four will be riding back. As I said, he's good with a gun."

Lomax grunted. "I don't think I need three helpers to take care of one man, but you're paying, so it's your deal. When do I get the fifty?"

Smiley reached into his pocket and brought out a fifty-dollar bill. He placed it in front of Lomax. "Right now."

"When do we leave?"

"Tomorrow morning at dawn. I don't want to go back to Pueblo. I figure Cully might get a sheriff and deputy to help him. I want to draw him out. Then it will be just us against him."

Lomax's fingers closed on the bill, like a crab closing on a prey. "I don't know the man, but I appreciate him. He's going to make me a lot of money." He stuck the bill into his shirt pocket. "Where do we meet tomorrow?"

"In front of the hotel."

Lomax nodded. "See you then."

As he walked away, two other men walked up. One had a red scar on his jaw. The other an aquiline nose that made him resemble a bird of prey.

"You must be the Anderson brothers," Smiley said.

"Yes. Luke and Abe. Hear you need men."

"Not just any men. I need men who know how to use guns and don't mind getting their hands messy. The pay is two hundred dollars. Fifty upfront, and the rest when a man named Cully is dead."

"Those are good wages. Count us in."

Smiley took two fifties from his shirt pocket and gave one to each of the men. "We meet tomorrow morning in front of the hotel. We're riding toward Pueblo, but I don't want to kill Cully there, though. I want to draw him away from the town. If we trade bullets in the town, the sheriff and deputy and probably a few townsfolk will join him. So I want him alone. I want to kill him and leave his body for the buzzards. That would be a fitting end for him."

"What you do with his body doesn't concern us. We'll just help you kill him. The rest is up to you," Luke Anderson said. He slipped the fifty into his pocket. "We'll see you at the hotel tomorrow."

"After we get the job done, I have another offer for you. It'll be a profitable one. But first things first."

The two men nodded.

"By the way are you all wanted anywhere?" Smiley said.

"Only in two states. And one of them is Texas, but that's a long way from here. No Colorado lawman is looking for us."

Smiley nodded. "Good, see you tomorrow."

He lit a cigar and waited for the fourth man that he expected. He took a deep puff and smiled. In spite of all the problems Cully had caused, things were looking up. He had hired three good men. When the Coyote arrived, he would make it four. Six men altogether, counting him and Palmer. Cully's days were numbered. And the number was less than double-digits.

Thirty minutes went by before the tall man with the blond mustache walked in. He had startling blue eyes. The man stared at the world maliciously. He gave off a smell of ruthlessness. Smiley was ruthless himself and a hard man. But the blue-eyed man made even him a bit nervous. Smiley had an edgy feeling, like there was no telling what the blue-eyed stranger would do. He might sign up after Smiley gave his pitch, or he might just draw and put a bullet through him.

Smiley coughed, then nodded at the man. "I'm Smiley. You looking for me?"

"Yep. I'm Coyote Rankin."

"You're called the blue-eyed wolf."

"That's one of the nicer names. Of course, those men who called me the nastier names to my face are not talking any more. They're pushing up daisies."

"I need to hire a man like you. I want a man killed. You won't have to do it alone. There be four other men in the gang. It should be easy, and the money is good."

"Four other men? Whoever you want dead can only be killed once. Why the other four men?"

"Because the man I want dead is named Cully, and he's quick and deadly. From time to time he has worn a badge on his chest. We might get lucky and put him away with one shot, but if we don't, then the other four men might be needed. Cully has considerable skills… and perhaps a bit of luck too."

Rankin snickered and shook his head. "Luck don't matter when you're facing lead. Your telegram said two hundred. That still good?"

"It is." Smiley held up a fifty-dollar bill. "Upfront money," he said, as he placed the bill on the table.

Rankin's fingers grabbed the bill. He looked at the seated man. "Smiley? Think I heard of you."

"Good, although I'm sure my reputation doesn't match yours." It was one of the few times Smiley had ever been modest in his life.

"It's good enough. It's said you're smart—and mean," Rankin said.

Smiley sipped more of his drink. "I'm smart all the time, but I'm mean when I have to be."

"Will anybody be with this man Cully?"

"No. He works alone. I can't be sure, but I think he'll be riding out solitary when he meets us."

"That will make it easier." Rankin thought for a moment. "Two hundred dollars for each man, and you have four men. That's a lot of money for one lawman."

"Killing Cully is worth every cent of it. It may cost a lot to kill him, but he cost me a lot of money, so I have a hankering to make sure he's dead. He's pledged to kill me and said he'd even pay for the funeral. I'm not that generous. I ain't going to bury him or pay for the funeral. The birds and the worms are going to eat him."

Rankin rested his hand on his pistol. "Cully, huh? Seems like I heard that name too. Was he the man who took in Simon Murdock not too long ago? Murdock swore to kill any lawman who came after him. But Cully had him draped over a saddle, and Murdock wasn't saying much."

"That was probably Cully. Sounds like him. Still want to sign up?"

Rankin laughed. "Of course. The fact that he got lucky one time doesn't mean a bullet will miss him this time. I'm in."

"Meet me at the hotel tomorrow morning and we'll head out."

CHAPTER 11

A soft rain was changing the dirt on the Pueblo streets to mud as Sheriff Hagin watched the two men ride slowly through the town. He stood outside his office with his deputy, Dick Holton. The rain padded against the wood as well as splattering the two riders. The two men had a serious look. Their hats protected most of their faces against the rain. One had a day-old beard. The other was clean-shaven. To the sheriff, the two didn't look like ordinary cowhands.

"Holton, what were the names of the gunmen Palmer said he sent for?"

"Dan Ballows and Ringo Starke."

The riders passed by the two men. Hagin pointed at them. "Do those two look like gunmen to you?"

Holton frowned. "Well, I could be wrong, but I'd take a guess they're up to no good, and it does appear they're heading for the hotel."

"Which would mean they had received telegrams from Palmer."

"That it would. Should we ride out there and let Cully knew he should be expecting company?"

"I don't think so. I imagine he's keeping an eye on the streets. He'll know they're here and be getting ready," Hagin said.

"Should we mosey up there to give him some help?"

"I have confidence in Cully. He works alone and probably doesn't need help." Hagin had been leaning against the building, but he took a step out into the street. "But I guess it wouldn't hurt to mosey on down. Never can tell."

———————

The front door of the boarding house opened into a room full of chairs and two sofas sitting on a thick carpet. To the left was a ragged bar but no bottles or glasses sat on it. A long mirror was behind it. Cully had his Sharps rifle, but he thought a short gun would be better in the closed environment. He eased down into a cushioned chair and crossed his legs. He put his hand on his pistol. He wore a red shirt with a vest that hid his deputy's badge. A blue bandana was tied at his throat.

One man banged on the door then opened it. Ballows and Starke walked in. Both were burly men. Ballows had a large nose and large lips. Starke looked at the world through beady black eyes. He looked around the building. His eyes blinked. He wasn't sure he liked what he saw. They stopped when they were about ten steps from Cully.

"You Smiley?" Starke asked.

"No. Mr. Smiley is not here."

The two gave questioning looks to each other. "A man named Palmer set us a telegram. Where is he?" Ballows asked.

"Mr. Palmer is in jail. He'll be there for a long time."

"Who are you?" Ballows said, the anger rising in his voice.

Cully gave a big smile. "Oh, I didn't tell you? Where are my manners? I'm a deputy. Name is Cully." He lifted the vest and let the two men see his badge. "Now why don't you two drop your guns and come down to the jail with me. We can provide you with three good meals a day. At no charge."

"We haven't done anything," Starke said.

"The wanted posters on you say differently." Cully's fingers wrapped around his pistol. "Unbuckle your gun belts and let them drop to the floor."

"Palmer betrayed us!" Ballows yelled.

"Guess you could say that."

"We'll kill him." Ballows went for his gun. "Right after we kill you."

In a split second, Cully pulled his gun from the holster and fired. The bullets caught Ballows in the side. He groaned, twisted in the air, and fell to the floor. Cully leaped from the chair and rolled when he hit the carpet, firing a third time at Starke. Starke had fired back, but the bullets tore into the soft fabric of the chair. As Starke leaped behind a sofa, Cully's next shot slit his leg, spilling blood on the dusty carpet.

Ballows yelled with pain. He stuck his hand over the wound. "Starke, I'm hit!"

"So am I."

"Toss your guns out. We can get you a good doctor at the jail. Here, you'll just die in pain. Toss them out!"

Ballows ignored the command. He lifted the gun and tried to aim it. But his hand wavered.

"Don't be a fool," Cully shouted.

Starke fired another bullet at Cully, but the lead whistled over his head. Ballows struggled to his knees. He cursed Cully and fired again, but his hand wasn't steady. The bullet hit the chair. Cully's next bullet caught him in the heart. Ballows dropped his gun and followed it to the floor.

"Want to surrender? It's one to one now," Cully shouted.

"No, I want to kill you!" came the reply. Starke fired again, but the bullet plunked into fabric.

"I'm going to watch when they hang you high."

Starke turned and looked at the door. With his partner gone, he didn't like the odds. He wanted to get out, get on his horse, and make a getaway. He pulled bullets from his gun belt and slid them into his gun. He wanted it fully loaded. Pump some bullets at his gun-toting adversary and, while the man had his head down, run to the door and down the steps to his horse. It wasn't a great plan, he thought, but it was the best one he had.

He rose up and pumped four bullets toward Cully and a fifth one when he was halfway to the door. As his fingers torched the doorknob, Cully stood up, gun in hand. He fired three times. Starke opened the door and ran out. But instead of running down the steps, his legs became entangled. Three red holes appeared in his back. His legs refused to support him. He pitched forward into the dirt. His gun dropped two feet in front of him. He reached out to grab it. His fingers touched the metal and then stiffened. He sighed and died.

Cully walked outside and looked at the body. "I supposed shooting is better than hanging." He shook his head. "That's two more funerals I'll have to pay for." He reloaded his gun, clicking the bullets into the slots. "But it's worth it."

He walked to Starke and reached into his pants pocket. He pulled out a ten-dollar bill.

"Well, I'll be," he said. "You can pay for our own funeral. We don't want to burden the taxpayers, do we?

He dragged Starke over to a horse and slung the man over the saddle. He did the same with Ballows. He climbed on his horse, grabbed the reins of the other two mounts and trotted Samson toward town. He hummed a tune while he rode. His mother always sang or hummed "Amazing Grace" while working. He had picked it up as a child. He always liked the tune, and it was a fine song to sing at funeral.

He halted as he saw Sheriff Hagin and Deputy Holton riding toward him. He grinned and handed the reins to the sheriff.

"Got some bad guys for you," he said.

"Come down to the office, Cully. I'll need you to sign a statement. These two men are wanted and probably have a reward on them."

"Well, it would be nice if they were worth something. I think their reputations were a bit overblown. They were not that good nor that smart."

"That's the key to living a long life," the sheriff said. "Get in a gunfight with men who are not very good with guns."

Cully laughed.

At his office, Sheriff Hagin took down the two wanted posters. "Won't need these anymore," he said.

Before he threw them away, he walked outside where the two dead men were still slung over the horses. With the poster in one hand, he grabbed the hair of an outlaw and pulled his head up. He compared it with the poster picture, then nodded.

"Yes, that's you. You're uglier than the poster, but it's you." He followed the same procedure with the second outlaw. Then nodded. "Holton, take these two over to the funeral home. Tell Mr. Willis he has some business."

Cully took out the ten-dollar bill and give it to the deputy. "Give him this. I found it in the pocket of one of the outlaws. They can pay for their own funerals."

Holton grabbed the bills and the horses' reins and started toward the funeral home.

"Like a cup of coffee, Cully?" the sheriff said.

"Sure, I'll take one."

They sat down in the office. The sheriff leaned back and put his boots on the desk. "What is your plan now? Smiley is still on the loose. You plan to go after him?"

Cully shook his head. "Not at all. I'm not going to go find him. I'm going to wait and have him come for me."

"How do you figure to work that?"

"I sent Mr. Smiley a telegraph that probably left him frowning. I tossed in a few insults and told him I'd enjoy seeing him hang. I signed it with Palmer's name knowing that Smiley might have been expecting some telegrams from his outlaw friend. Also indicated I'd be at the hotel."

"You're setting yourself up as a target?"

"I'm already a target. Smiley will want revenge for me killing his friends and taking the two women, both of whom are safely on their way back to their hometown." Cully sipped his coffee. "But I don't think Smiley wants any more trouble here. His scheme has been uncovered. You and your deputy will be on the lookout for him. He has to go someplace else, but I'm sure that first he wants to take care of me. I'm at his house. I figure he'll send someone with a challenge. He'll say he wants to have it out with me. Man to man. Gun against gun."

"But Smiley doesn't like to fight fire. He'll have other men with him."

"No doubt. A robber and a murderer would not be opposed to lying about a fair fight. I'm sure he has a few men with him, but he'll have to let me know where he is. I'll find him and pick the time when I go get him." He chuckled. "I just made some more money when those two outlaws wanted to fight it out. I wonder how much Smiley is paying his men to kill me."

"Probably a lot," the sheriff said.

"I kinda wonder how much my life is worth."

The sheriff sipped his coffee. "You're gonna find out real soon."

"Guess I am. Durango is not that far away. Shouldn't be too long before riders get here."

"You could just walk away, Cully. Smiley ain't going to use that house he thought would bring him a fortune. Most lawmen turn a blind eye to such houses, and some are in towns that won't allow them. But what Smiley was planning was close to slavery, and I'd shut it down. I don't know how he thought he'd get away with it. But honest men never can figure out the mind of an outlaw much less a man like Smiley. If he wants to start something like that, he'll have to find another town. You've done your job. As I said, you can walk away."

"No, I can't. I've got a hunch Smiley wants me dead. He'll be coming after me. So I might as well make it easy for him and me. No use dragging things out. So I think I'll get some lunch, buy a bottle, and wait. I'll grab a book so I can read while I'm waiting."

"You can read?"

"Sure can. Momma was very big on education. I was in school by the time I was seven, and I could read before that. Momma taught me. We were not dirt poor. We had enough food and clothes and a little left over. I had a great childhood. Momma always liked books in the house. She read them to me until I had enough learning to read them myself." He gave a big smile. "You know what she told me once?"

"That you'd be shooting bad guys?"

Cully chuckled and nodded. "Almost. She read to me about King Arthur and his knights and told me I'd be a knight. Told me about Lancelot." He raised his coffee cup. "I have the strength of ten because my heart is pure."

The sheriff showed a sardonic grin. "That's wonderful, my friend. But while a pure heart is admirable, it won't stop bullets. So you be careful. When that rider comes in if you need help..."

"That's all right, Sheriff. I usually work alone. But then, so did Lancelot." He sipped from the coffee cup. "By the way, how much reward money is on Smiley's head? Since I might say hello to him soon, I'm a little curious about that."

The sheriff smiled. "I checked on that today. He's worth eight hundred dollars, dead or alive."

"Well, I'll see if he'd like to come in alive, but I kind of doubt that. I think he will want to make a last stand. But... we'll see."

"I'm going to make my rounds. If you decide you want help, let me know."

———————

Cully walked down the street to the saloon and purchased a bottle of whiskey. He carried the bottle to the livery stable where he had left Samson for the night. The owner had promised a good rubdown for the horse and several ripe apples. Samson did appear brushed. His coat almost shone when Cully walked in.

The owner waved at him. "Samson has been fed, groomed, and washed, Mr. Cully. That's a fine horse you have there."

"Yes, he is." Cully lifted the saddle and placed it on Samson's back.

"Be gone long, Mr. Cully?"

"Oh, think I'll be out for a while, sir. Then I'll be back, and Samson can enjoy more of your hospitality."

"My business always welcomes guests," the hostler laughed.

CHAPTER 12

Cully rode to the hotel and found a shady place for Samson to stay. He strode out to the porch and sat down, extending his legs to a railing. He placed a glass on the small table beside him and poured liquor into it. Opening a book, he smiled. He liked to roam but he could also relax and be patient. He opened a tobacco pouch and rolled a cigarette then opened the book.

He was still reading when the lone rider came toward him. He rode slowly, looking around, as if he were edgy, wondering if a lawman might show up. The man was an outlaw, Cully thought. He had tracked enough men down to spot them. The stranger smoked a cigar; the smoke trailed behind him as his horse trotted to the house. Cully noticed the man had bright blue eyes. The man halted his horse at the porch and pulled the cigar from his mouth.

"You Cully?"

"Since the day I was born."

"Was told you'd be here."

"Smiley tell you that?"

The man nodded.

"He smiling much anymore? The last I saw him, he was grouchy and frowning."

"I'll tell you where you can see him again. He sent me to give you a message."

"So you're Smiley's messenger boy."

The stranger gritted his teeth. "I don't like that term," Rankin said. "Why don't you take it back?"

Cully ignored him. "Smiley was too afraid to come? Maybe if you rode with him and held his hand..."

"He has his reasons. Besides, he's got bad memories of this town."

"I imagine he's got bad memories of me too. Sort of sad. I always think fondly of him," Cully said, drinking more of his liquor.

"Mister, you've got an odd sense of humor."

Cully said nothing. He just stared at the stranger.

"Something bothering you, Cully?" The voice held a note of hostility.

"Nope, not at all. I was just trying to remember something. Heard rumors of a blue-eyed scoundrel when I was down Waco way. Had an interesting name—Coyote Rankin. That you?"

"That's me."

"So what are you doing up this way? Waco, that's down near the border. Long trip up here."

Rankin leaned on his saddle. "I'm getting paid well."

"What are you supposed to do for the money?"

Rankin's voice became cold. "Help kill you."

"Hope you are getting paid well. That's gonna be a tough job."

Rankin's hand slid toward his holster.

Cully touched his gun too. He smiled. "You want to try that now."

Rankin stiffened but then slid his hand away from his waist. "No, I can wait. Besides, Smiley wants to kill you personally. He just wanted a few men to back him up. Not that I'm supposed to tell you that. He wanted you to think it would be one on one."

"I wouldn't be that stupid, but it doesn't matter. I'll still meet him. Since you're the messenger you need to tell me where he is."

"At the entrance to Horseshoe Canyon. He'll be waiting for you."

"Tell him I'll be there. How much is he paying you?"

"None of your business. That's between Smiley and me."

Cully tossed his cigarette away. "A dead man can't pay you anything. You should think about that. You should ride away. Go back to Waco."

Rankin's voice remained cold. "Thanks for the advice. Here's what I think of it." He leaned over and spit on the ground. "I'll see you at the canyon," he said.

"You sure will," Cully said.

As Rankin rode away, Cully walked down the steps of the house and planted his boots in the dirt. He grinned as he thought that he should have asked the blue-eyed bandit how many men Smiley had. Not that Rankin would have told him. Cully guessed about three or four. Call it four, count Smiley, and that makes the odds five to one. And he didn't think, even with five to one odds, that Smiley wanted a fair fight. He turned his gaze toward the sky. It was a few minutes past noon. The orange sun was high in the sky. He looked east.

Horseshoe Canyon was about eight miles in that direction. The entrance of the canyon faced west. That might be to his advantage, Cully thought. In the evening, given the angle of the sun, the light might shine in the eyes of Cully's gang, but he would have the sun at his back.

Calling the place a canyon was a slight exaggeration, Cully thought. Horseshoe Canyon wasn't as large as most places called canyons. If he remembered correctly, the canyon was shot full of small caves. If I were Smiley, Cully thought, I'd place a man in one of those caves, or better yet, two men in two of those caves. They could cover the mouth of the canyon from their rock perches. Any cowboy riding in would be an easy target.

Might be wise to come in the back way, he thought. Circle around. Crawl though the rocks and sneak into a cave after first pinpointing where the snipers were. Get them first and then say hello to Smiley.

He had walked to Samson. He petted the mount. "What do you think of that idea, Sam? Think it might be worthwhile."

He lifted his rifle from the saddle and looked it over. It was fine. He pulled his pistol from his holster and did another check. Pistol was fine too. He lifted his canteen and took a long drink.

He needed to put together a plan. A frontal approach was dangerous. Smiley wasn't known for fair fights. Cully knew he might be dead when he got within rifle range. He could sneak up on the gang. Get within pistol range before they realized he was near. It would be difficult with guards in caves who had a good view of the road in, but it could be done. He took another drink from the canteen. He patted Samson again.

"Sam, sometimes you have to be flexible. I usually work alone, but perhaps I should call for reinforcements in this case." Samson nodded and neighed in reply. "Looks like you agree with me. I always said horses were smart. It might not be too wise to take on five men alone. Especially when I'm guessing those men have wanted posters on them. A few sheriffs might like the chance to take those outlaws in... or kill them. But how do we get to the canyon alive, and how do we get out of it alive?"

Samson neighed again but had no answers.

"But I've put together plans before. It'll come to me. However, since I am officially a deputy, I might..."

He thought for a minute as the details for his assault on Smiley and his gang came to him. He shifted through the ideas, accepted some and rejected others. He was a fearless man but not a reckless one. Taking on five men might be called reckless. No matter how brave you are, if you are reckless, you go into an early grave. He preferred to live a long life. He also knew he wanted a family. A wife. And sons and daughters.

There had always been a desire for a family in him. He had a very happy family life as a child and wanted a family as an adult too. The desire was always dormant in him. But now, after seeing Kane and Miss Thomas, it had strengthened. The two young people looked so happy after narrowly escaping disaster.

He gave a knowing grin. That was the one problem with Lancelot. He should have married and stayed in love with his own wife. He wouldn't have been glancing at the Queen.

But, as his mother would say, sin can mess up the finest Camelot.

Forty-five minutes later he had the details of his plan in place. It wasn't perfect. What plan ever was? But he thought it would work. There was one aspect that he had no control over. He had to trust when he rode toward Smiley's gang, the outlaw would want to look him in the eye before firing. If Smiley wanted one of his sharpshooters to pick Cully from the saddle before he got in pistol range then... then the undertaker could write, "Bad Planner," on his tombstone. He needed to talk to Sheriff Hagin and then he would make sure Smiley got to the cemetery on time.

CHAPTER 13

Most of the miles to the canyon were desolate. Flat land for almost five miles. The wind howled as Cully started his trip. The emptiness of the blue sky and the openness of the land showed how barren Colorado could be. The wind blew sand toward him and Samson. Cully tied his red kerchief around his face, protecting his cheeks, nose, and mouth. He rubbed Samson's neck.

"Sorry I don't have anything to protect you, Samson. But you do have a tough hide."

For some reason, the emptiness increased the ache of loneliness. The idea of a family came into his mind again. The barrenness of the land reminded him of the barrenness of his own life. If he was killed in a blazing gun battle with Smiley and his gang, who would mourn for him? He had friends—two good friends who had both fought with him— and acquaintances among numerous sheriffs and deputies, but who would care with that special kind of love for him? If your life is spent fighting to preserve what is good and noble, you should have someone special you're fighting for, he thought.

The love between Kane and Miss Thomas had touched him deeply. He had been invited to their wedding. At first he thought he would decline. He didn't like the East and he didn't like cities. Too many people were crowded in together. Despite the barrenness of some of Colorado and most of Wyoming, a state he had also lived in, open spaces were where he felt most at home. But he did prefer forests to the barren land. However, he had changed his mind about the wedding. He would attend after all. He wanted to see the loving couple married. It would be a joyous occasion and he wanted to share it. The thought of it eased the aching in his heart.

The wind eased. So did the sting of the sand. Dark clouds, moving as fast as the Wyoming winds, formed and blackened the sky. Storms could gather quickly in Colorado, but many don't last too long. As he eased the kerchief down, he thought that might be an advantage in the coming fight. Rain could hurt the aim of some men. Not his, though. He was steady in rain or shine. But other men were not. He looked up, and the clouds grew darker. A silver lightning bolt split the gray skies. Thunder boomed in the darkness. That is a good sign. That's to my advantage, Cully thought. He would be at the mouth of the canyon around five. This time of year, there would still be plenty of light... but not with the storm. A storm could reduce visibility. A plus, he thought, a definite plus.

His mother had said she would always be praying for him. "Sam, her prayers are working today," he said aloud. He patted the horse. "You know, Sam, a lot of battles have been won or lost because of the weather. Maybe that will be true today too."

He spurred Samson forward.

———————

At the mouth of Horseshoe Canyon, Smiley paced impatiently. He didn't have a raincoat, so the droplets splattered on his shirt. The light rain attacked the campfire. The fires sputtered but didn't go out. He looked up at the cave where one of the Anderson brothers was posted. He saw nothing but knew the man had retreated into the cave to get out of the rain.

"Relax. The man I talked to didn't look like a man who would git scared and run the other way," Rankin said.

Smiley leaned against a large rock whose height came up to his waist. Droplets plunked on the rock, sending water through the air. "He ain't. Not Cully. He's coming. Just wish he would get here." He looked up. "Luke. Hey, Luke!"

Luke Anderson stepped out of a cave. He held a rifle and waved it.

"See anything?"

"Not yet."

Smiley kept pacing although the dirt was changing to mud. Lomax and Abe Anderson dashed under a clump of trees next to the campfire.

Lomax wiped several drops from his face. "I'd rather kill someone in the sun than in the rain," Lomax said.

"Maybe Cully won't show until it's sunny again," Abe Anderson said. "You know anything about that man?"

Lomax nodded. "Cully? I've heard his name. He's a loner, has been a state lawman and a U.S. Marshal. I've heard its best not to tangle with him."

"Looks like you didn't take that advice."

"For this kind of money, no. It's said Cully talks straight and shoots straight. But few men are worth the money I'm getting, so I'm just going to shoot straight and shoot first. That should take care of Cully."

Luke Anderson's voice rang through the camp. "Smiley, there's a rider coming. Still in the distance. You can hardly see him, but he's headed this way."

Smiley peered down the trail. Through the rain, dark, and mist he barely made out a single rider: a tall man, riding slowly.

"That's him. It's got to be," Smiley said. "Get ready!"

———————

Samson's hooves now clumped down on mud as he trotted toward the camp. Cully tensed in the saddle. This was the time when a bullet might come his way. He breathed deeply and hoped Smiley wanted to gloat before ordering his men to fire. He looked up on the cliff, hoping to spot a sniper. He hoped there was only one. His plan only called for one. If Smiley had a different plan, a bullet would be whistling toward him in a few seconds.

Samson's hooves plopped on the mud. As he rode forward, Cully noticed four men in the distance, partially hidden in the darkness. One man stood in the center of the group. The other three men stood around him. He slowed Samson and halted the horse twenty feet from the men. From that distance he could see the huge, malicious grin on Smiley's face.

"Well, well. For a while I wasn't sure you'd come. You have guts, after all," Smiley said.

With a finger, Cully pushed back his hat. Then he placed his hand on his pistol. "I think all you men have posters on you. If you will just drop your guns, then there'll be no trouble."

A huge laugh came from Smiley. Several of his men joined in. "You're a fool, Cully, but I guess you're a confident fool. Drop our guns?" Smiley said. "You figure you got us surrounded?"

Cully nodded. "Yes. If you drop your guns, you'll soon be in a jail cell instead of a coffin. It's up to you."

Smiley eased his hand toward his holster...

———————

Luke Anderson stepped slowly through the mud. He eased down to a knee as he brought the rifle to his shoulder. Rain patted on his back. He grinned as he put his finger on the trigger. Nothing was easier than killing a man on a horse standing still. Light was dim, but there was enough to take a shot. The man called Cully was in his gunsight. When Smiley shouted the order...

Then he felt the gun barrel on the back of his neck.

"I'd put that down if I were you," Sheriff Hagin said.

When there was no response, Hagin jabbed Anderson's neck. "Let it drop. I won't tell you again."

Anderson loosened his grip on the rifle and dropped it in the mud.

———————

Cully yelled to make sure he was heard over the wind. "Your business is finished, Smiley. The sheriff knows about it in Pueblo. The house you used will be put to the torch soon. You're finished." He looked at the gang members. "I don't know what he promised you, but he can't pay. His business was shut down, and he's broke."

"That's not true. I can pay you. Don't listen to him!"

On the cliff, Sheriff Hagin leaned forward to hear the conversation in the camp. Seeing his attention was briefly diverted, Anderson swung his arm around, knocking the rifle in Hagin's hand. As he slipped and tumbled to the ground, Hagin's finger pulled the trigger.

Cully and the gang members looked up. Smiley went for his gun.

"Kill him!" Smiley yelled.

Before Smiley spoke the last syllable Cully whipped out his pistol and fired. Rankin had managed to get his gun out of his holster when the bullet ripped into his shoulder. He groaned but held onto his gun. Cully spun Samson around. As the horse galloped back down the path, Cully leaped into the forest. He thudded on the ground then rolled immediately, picking up wet grass and leaves on his back. Bullets whizzed by him and skimmed the bark of two surrounding trees. Behind a rock, he rose up and fired.

Abe Anderson was slow and caught in the open. Two bullets crashed into his stomach. He gasped and fell down to his knees on the muddy, wet ground. As blood dripped into the mud, he stretched out a hand to catch himself when he fell. His hand hit the ground, but the arm was too weak to support him. His face plunged into the mud.

Hagin reacted quickly when Luke Anderson charged him. He lifted his foot and planted a large boot into Anderson's stomach then leaped up. As Anderson stumbled on weakened legs, Hagin swung his rifle around. The barrel caught the outlaw in the jaw, knocking blood and skin into the rain and wind. The blow knocked Anderson several steps toward the precipice. He threw his arms back and tried to regain his stability. But Hagin's powerful second kick knocked him over the edge. He yelled as he fell into space and was still yelling when he slammed into the mud.

Smiley, behind a tree, fired repeatedly toward Cully. Rankin and Lomax had also taken cover. Smiley saw Luke Anderson fall from the crag and knew Abe had been mortally wounded. He cursed, knowing he only had three men left, and he was facing two men. Suddenly he didn't like the odds. Lately, things had begun to go wrong. He looked toward the horses. A bullet pinged on the rock he was using for cover. Smiley ducked and gripped his gun tighter.

Rankin fired at Sheriff Hagin, but Hagin had moved away from the cliff's edge. Bullets whizzed harmlessly past him. He threw himself on the ground and crawled forward to the edge.

Lomax didn't mind the odds, but he didn't like the positions. Instead of a gang member being above them, a friend of Cully's had the high ground. He knew he was vulnerable. The cliff shooter had the better angle on them. He kept looking over his shoulder while looking for Cully outside the camp. If the shooter would stand up and give him a target... But the shooter didn't.

"Toss your guns out!" Cully yelled. "I'm out here, and there's a man behind you. We have you trapped."

"I'll kill you!" Smiley yelled. He rapidly fired three bullets toward Cully, but they hit the rock. Smiley knew he had to reload. He wanted a rifle. He knew a bullet from a handgun couldn't reach the high ledge. But his rifle was on his horse, about twenty feet away. The horses stomped their feet nervously, due to the noise. Smiley had three bullets left in his handgun. He emptied his gun at Cully then ran toward his horse. As he ran, he felt the pain and burning as Cully's bullet thunked into the meaty part of his thigh. He yelled in pain, tried to put his foot on the ground, but the leg gave way, and he crashed into the earth. "Help! Help!"

No one moved. The other two outlaws didn't want to risk getting shot for Smiley. They were beginning to think they had made a bad deal.

Lomax aimed for Cully again. He thought if he moved to the right, he might have a better angle. But he would have to be quick. He stepped quickly to the right but not quickly enough. His gun spit bullets at Cully but as he dove back, a rifle bullet blasted his side. The impact knocked him to the ground. As he struggled to get up, Hagin fired rapidly. One bullet twanged into the bush beside Lomax but the second landed solidly in his chest, just below the heart. His heart beat for several seconds more but fell silent.

Coyote Rankin wore two guns. He said nothing but grabbed both of them and started walking toward Cully, firing both weapons. Bullets skimmed off the rock Cully was behind. He shook his head. He thought Rankin's charge was near suicidal. He leaped up and fired at almost point blank range at the outlaw. His bullets lodged in the man's chest, leaking blood. Rankin was out of bullets but he kept pulling the triggers. The only noise heard were clicks. He fell backward and landed in the road. Cully walked up to him. The bright blue eyes grew dim as Rankin turned his head to the side and took one last breath.

Cully ran toward the camp. Limping, Smiley stumbled toward his horse. He had managed to grab the reins when Cully called to him. "Drop the gun! It's all over."

Smiley looked back and stared with bitter hatred at Cully. He carried a derringer in his pocket, and he silently swore that the last thing he would do on earth would be to kill the deputy. He raised his hand and dropped the gun. "I'm wounded. I surrender," he said. He held onto his horse and saddle so he could stand up.

Cully looked up and saw Hagin was hastening down from the cliff.

"I give up. You won," Smiley said, then smiled as Cully moved closer. The derringer had a very limited range. He needed Cully to walk a few more steps before a bullet could reach him.

"You are bad news, Smiley. A lot of men have died around you."

Smiley gritted his teeth. Pain shot through his body from the wound in his leg. "There's time for one more," he said.

He whipped out the derringer. Cully wasn't surprised. He never thought Smiley would surrender. He brought his gun up.

Smiley groaned as the bullet entered his stomach. The second bullet brought no sound. Smiley slipped down to his knees in the mud, dropped the derringer, and died.

Hagin walked toward the camp, rifle in hand. He stood and looked down at Smiley. "The wages of sin..." he said.

"Are your picture on a poster and death," Cully said.

EPILOGUE

The wedding had all the white lace and pink bridal dresses that such an occasion demands. Cully, sitting in the back row, smiled as he heard the organ music. It was the first time in years he had heard an organ play. Considering his recent adventures, he was happy the organist wasn't playing a funeral dirge. The wedding was a much happier occasion.

He recognized the groom standing beside the minister at the front of the church. Sherman Kane looked ecstatic.

Cully was not at home in the East surrounded by church splendor. The organist changed tunes and played "Here Comes the Bride" as Susie walked down the aisle. She was a beautiful bride. Her smile had the radiance of the sun. Her eyes gleamed with happiness. The white dress shone as it reflected the lights in the church. She eased slowly down the aisle. When she passed the pew where Cully sat, she blew him a kiss.

Cully spotted the parents of Kane. He had talked briefly with them before sitting in the pew. The man was tall, somewhat stout, and had a mustache and almost a military bearing. The wife was five inches shorter than her husband but an attractive woman with reddish-brown hair. The couple did not look happy but, Cully thought, did not look unhappy either. They appeared to be ready to give the marriage a chance without passing judgment on it.

Susie stopped when she reached the altar and smiled at the delighted groom. The minister opened his arms as if greeting the congregants.

Cully beamed with happiness as the ceremony continued. Maybe, he thought, he really was a knight. His mother would have been proud of him for rescuing Miss Thomas from Smiley and his gang. In the recent past there had been violence, but in this church there was peace, gentleness, and joy. That was the key, he thought. He knew violence was a part of his work. Wanted men and outlaws did not go peacefully to the local jail. They had to be forced. But if had to fire his pistol or rifle, the enjoyment of the job was not in shooting or violence, but from protecting the innocent and keeping the West a decent place to live.

"By the authority vested in me by the state of Pennsylvania, I now pronounce you man and wife," the pastor said.

After the couple departed, the congregants mingled briefly. Cully heard one woman say, "What a beautiful ceremony."

And it was.

At the reception, Cully picked up a cup of pink punch. It didn't have the bite of whiskey, but it was very good. As he sipped it, he knew just as Sherman Kane looked comfortable and at ease in a city in the East, he wasn't. He could stand a city for a few days, but it wasn't the life for him. He was a man of the West.

He smiled as he saw Kane's father approach him. The man extended his hand. "You are Mr. Cully?"

"I am."

"Kane told me how you helped both him and Susie. I just wanted to personally extend my thanks. I can't express how much my wife and I appreciate what you did. What you did took courage and integrity."

"I was happy to help. Your son is a good man. Your daughter-in-law is a fine and courageous woman."

The man swallowed and nodded. "Yes, I think she is. I think my wife and I had a blind spot at first. To our sorrow, I think we contributed to the problem. Now we have welcomed Susie into our family."

"I'm glad to hear that."

"Mr. Cully, I don't want to talk business at this event, but I'm a businessman, and I'm always looking for investments. My son told me how much he likes the West—although he only saw it very briefly—and said there might be many investment opportunities out there."

"I'm sure there are. The West is a booming area. There are always financial opportunities in such areas."

"If you see one, let me know. A ranch, a farm, a factory. Both my son and daughter-in-law like horses. If you see a horse ranch for sale or anything like that, send me a letter, and I'll look into it."

Cully nodded. "I will."

"Thank you. Again, my appreciation."

As the man walked back to his wife, Cully saw the newlyweds walking toward him.

"Cully, so glad you could make it. Thank you for coming," Kane said.

"You're welcome. I come east every couple of years." He raised his glass. "I do enjoy the pink punch."

"Why don't you stay around?" Susie said. "We'd love to keep you here in the East."

"That's true," Kane said. "My family runs several businesses. There would definitely be a place for a man with your talents. The salary would be good. You'd make a lot more than you would as a deputy or a sheriff."

Cully smiled. "I'm sure I would, and I thank you, but the East is not for me. Many people belong here. This is the place they should be. But I belong in the West. My life is out there, and it's a very good life. I wouldn't trade it for the world. I've got a train ticket for the evening train. I'll have a good night's sleep and be close to home tomorrow morning."

"I understand and wish you well, but we'll miss you," Kane said.

"Thank you for that. But as a man of the West, this is the time to say farewell."

The End

Could I get you to consider leaving a review on Amazon? Thanks.

ABOUT THE AUTHOR:

Orris Slade writes westerns. Written from a down-to-earth, gritty perspective, these tales are meant to entertain and captivate readers. Orris originates from Oregon and now hangs his hat in Montana.

Stay in touch....more westerns are on the way.

Email: Orris.Slade@gmail.com

OTHER BOOKS BY
ORRIS SLADE

Watch for "Cully – Justice Served" to be released soon.

32569271R00073

Made in the USA
Middletown, DE
05 January 2019